Books by Donna Bocks

Lavender Blues
Came to Say Good-bye
Heartbeat of Home
Purple Prairie Schooner
Texas Tango
Twin Trees
Thunder Ridge
Squatters Corner

Squatters Corner

Donna Bocks

BIRTH A BOOK
PUBLICATION SERVICES
A DIVISION OF
OPEN WINDOW CREATIONS

Squatters Corner

By Donna Bocks
Published by Open Window Creations
Copyright © 2013 by Donna Bocks
ISBN: 978-0-9802090-9-9

Project Development: Open Window Creations LLC
Editorial Services: Pam Suwinsky
Cover and Book Design: Greystroke Creative
Administrative Manager: Nichol Skaggs
Printed in the United States of America

Copies of Squatter's Corner may be ordered from:
www.lulu.com/spotlight/donnabocks
www.amazon.com
Kindle - www.amazon.com
Nook - www.barnesandnoble.com/c/donna-bocks
www.donnabocks.wordpress.com
DonnaBocks@gmail.com

Dedication

I dedicate Squatters Corner
to my kind and helpful publishing assistants

*Nichol Skaggs
and Linda Vander Leek*

Acknowledgment

*Thank you, Dr. Dennis E Hensley and Pam Suwinsky,
for your hard work, competent corrections, and helpful ideas.
Your editorial services have made my stories worth reading!*

CHAPTER 1

Squatters Corner, Montana
Sunday, March 18, 2012

Randy Tabano was in the bathroom when he heard the spitting, sputtering, gurgling. The teakettle was capable of a whistle, but he had filled it too full. It sounded like it was dying.

In his haste to get into his old gray sweats before heading into the kitchen, he nearly pitched head-first into the tub. It was his second day at the cabin. He saw no improvement over his blunders of the previous days.

Hustling toward the sound, he reached the stove and removed the kettle from the burner. At the same time he jerked open a cupboard door, grabbing a mug and the small jar of instant coffee. "They sure keep everything neat and tidy. I'll have to shape up. Great. I'm talking to myself already."

He couldn't believe he had slept in. Usually he was up at six. At the sliding door he looked up at the mountains. His eyes moved down to get another view of the stream that passed about thirty-five yards from the seemingly new deck. The yard slanted enough for him to see the water bubbling over the rocks.

Randy stopped as if in a trance. Close to the stream was a faded green Adirondack chair. In it sat a young woman. He looked away, then back. She was really there. During the night there had been a dusting of snow, he hoped for the last time this year. Everything was covered, but the early morning sun and stillness of the air made it appear warm.

The woman was wearing knee-high leather boots; a plaid blanket-type cape was draped partially over her shoulder. Her clothing appeared to have been made just for her. Her face was soft, lovely and delicate. Her makeup was perfect. One thing seemed to be missing: her personality. It seemed closely guarded like it was being held back, to be revealed when she thought a person was trustworthy.

As she turned toward Randy her long blonde hair blew aside. The eyes, that's what puzzled him. She looked at him casually as if she had expected to see him there. The faintest of smiles seemed to convey complete recognition.

Small communities do not keep secrets about new faces, and the word about Randy had been creeping around Squatters Corner for about a week. A man from the city like Randy would not be aware of this characteristic of small towns; if he did he wouldn't have been surprised when the woman observed him as if he was someone she already knew.

Very slowly he pushed the slider open in fear that she would vanish. She remained. Lifting his mug, steam rising as it caught up with the cold air, he suggested, "Coffee?"

Her smile broadened a bit. "No, thanks. Just on my way to church. This is the best spot for listening to the mountains. I couldn't resist the pause." She wrapped herself up warmly and walked away.

He called after her. "Maybe another time?" She didn't turn around but waved her hand.

Randy watched until she disappeared among the trees along the stream. Sliding the door shut, he turned and moved to another window. Then he raced to the second floor. Yes, there were footprints in the snow. Who was she?

• • •

Moving down the stairs, at a slower pace, he tried to reorganize his thoughts. When he got to the kitchen he spotted a note.

> *Frank called. I had limited time to freshen the place up. Set in a few food supplies to get you started. You have arrived at the most beautiful place in the world.*
> *Welcome, Merry*

• • •

His mind was blank as to how he had spent Saturday.

He didn't know who this Merry was, but her efforts to welcome his arrival were appreciated, especially the eggs and other staples. He must look her up and thank her.

He had a quick bowl of cereal and milk, then settled at the table with two pieces of toast and peanut butter, and his second cup of coffee.

Shaking his head, as if to clear out cobwebs, he decided to start the day over again, to see if he could get things in perspective.

Things had changed so fast; maybe, he hoped, for the better. He sat back, realizing it was the first time he had felt relaxed in months. Heading for the desk, he returned with a yellow tablet and a pencil. Maybe if he jotted things down he could put his mind in order.

It was Sunday. Although Randy was not a steady churchgoer he was a strong believer. He tried to be the best person he could be, but for the past year or so, Sunday rest was not part of his agenda.

He was a professional writer, yet he couldn't seem to put his private feelings of pressure into words. It felt like the world was closing in on him, like he could see it moving toward him. He had begun to panic. He could shake it off for a few days. Then it would start again.

It was like being on a trip and losing his maps. He had never felt so lost, like he was wandering with no purpose.

He had begged God to help him to understand and to find a way out. "Am I talking to myself, God, or to you? What's happening to me?"

This morning the cloud in his mind lifted long enough for him to get a clear picture of the past few days.

• • •

On Wednesday of last week he'd been able to talk to Jill, his wife, about his confusion. She had put her arms around him, hugging him gently.

"Honey, how many times has Frank Avery insisted that you go to his cabin in Montana? Lately, whenever you run into him he brings it up. He's not only your boss, he's your best friend."

"I don't know. I'll see."

"No, it's time to make a move now. Maybe it will help." Jill had left the room and returned with the portable phone from the bedroom and Frank's work number at the newspaper. "Call now."

CHAPTER 2

Coeur d'Alene, Idaho
Thursday, March 15, 2012

At the Coeur d'Alene bus station there had been the busyness that accompanies travel. Randy was the last passenger to board. He turned to wave. Jill had waved in return and faked a smile. She felt like she was sending one of the children off alone for the first time.

Jill's long black silky hair was beginning to tumble. The pins were coming loose. She had worked hard on it this morning. Had he noticed? Come to think of it, had she even noticed what he had worn for his trip? All she remembered was that face that meant the world to her.

The pit of her stomach hurt. When she reached the car she fell apart. Knowing that crying wouldn't help did not shut off the water supply.

Feeling exhausted, she couldn't even dig in her purse for the car keys. She wondered if this was what Randy was experiencing: hopelessness? No wonder he was frightened. She needed him here with her. But she wanted him to be his old self. Neither of them understood the problem, nor the cause.

Jill felt a sensation of movement that startled her and she gripped the steering wheel. Then she realized that the car next to her was backing out of its parking space.

That jolted her back to reality. She took a deep breath. Fumbling for her car keys she discovered the folded note.

Jill,
I love you with all my heart.
I'll return as soon as I feel
strong again. Hug the kids.
Randy

The previous tears were a trickle. The note broke the dam. Her chest ached. She hoped they'd made the right decision. "Oh Randy!"

• • •

On Wednesday she and Randy had finally removed the barrier that had been building between them. "What's the matter, Randy? Is it me?"

"No, not at all. Jill, I love and cherish you and the kids." He had looked like he was going to break down. His eyes were full of misery. When he had relaxed his body he appeared ready to collapse.

"I don't know what it is. I seem to have no feelings or responses about anything."

"Maybe you should see a doctor."

"What do I do, just go in and say, 'I don't feel well'? I feel like I'm dying, or worse, like I've already gone. I hear people talking but their voices sound far away."

He had looked tired from the exertion of just expressing himself.

It was then she had insisted that he call Frank, his boss at the newspaper. The words were etched in her brain. "Frank has always said that getting away from the rat race, out of Idaho and into Montana was stimulating and refreshingly beautiful. The clear country air is great. It sort of sets things straight."

After he'd made the arrangements with Frank, Randy looked puzzled. "Am I so easily dispensable?"

Jill hoped she had looked strong and loving. "I need your strength in this household, my dear one, and I don't want you to ever forget that."

The kids had left for school. She had helped him pack. The two of them sat in the sunny breakfast nook having a cup of coffee. Jill remembered reaching for Randy's hand.

"I want you to promise a couple of things. Number one, you'll write us once a week. We will want a description of this special place, and let us know how you are doing. I'll write to you, but my news will be the old familiar.

"Number two, I want you back, Randy: strong and healthy. I want my man back and the children need their father."

• • •

In the car Jill pulled herself up straight. Patting her face with a soft tissue, she smiled. "This isn't helping, God. With your help we'll move ahead. Think positive. This will be the answer."

Heading the car toward home she shifted her mind to the fact that she was in charge at this end. Life needed to run as smoothly as possible. The transition would not be flawless.

She was exhausted physically and emotionally. Her purse landed on the kitchen counter and her body on the sofa, with her long legs tucked up behind her. She felt like someone had knocked her out with a baseball bat. The postman's jolly whistle as he clinked the lid of the mailbox awakened her. She felt the need to jump up in a hurry, but her body wouldn't cooperate.

Slowly she wandered into the bathroom. Looking into the mirror was a bad experience. Puffy red eyes instead of her usual hazel color stared back at her. A cold washcloth and fresh lipstick helped. Moving out to the yard to putter around in the sunshine might perk her up.

She was feeling better when Trish and Danny, thirteen and eleven, returned from school. She knew that her face was still slightly swollen, but the two knew enough about what was taking place to understand.

Tomorrow she would sit down and do some restructuring. Their everyday existence would be drastically different.

How long would the separation last? How would it change all of their lives? She'd plan on several months. If it were a shorter time, she would be more than happy to switch back to their previous ways.

That night, she held her slender fingers together like a church steeple and took up a long-forgotten habit.

"Now I lay me

Down to sleep. . . ."

CHAPTER 3

Squatters Corners
Monday, March 19, 2012

Leaving Coeur d'Alene, along Highway 90, Randy was oblivious to the life passing by the bus windows. He had chosen not to fly to Squatters Corner because the change would be so abrupt. He wanted to do some thinking, but about what? He felt only a numbness until the driver touched his shoulder and announced they had arrived in Livingston, Montana. It was Friday the sixteenth. He hadn't paid attention to details, and it was then he discovered that he had to travel by Short Way bus, on Highway 89, toward Great Falls to reach his destination. The ticket office informed him that that route was run only on Tuesdays and Thursdays.

Gathering his things, he went to the coffee shop feeling defeated. Why could he not function? He was explaining his situation to the waitress when a man a few stools down spoke up.

"I can help you. I am going through there. I'm on a time schedule so I have to drop you at the bus station."

Randy almost fell apart. "I will accept your offer, sir."

He arrived at the Squatters Corner bus station that same day. His recollections of that Friday were clear. It was dusk. A cold rain was splashing into puddles. His ride had set Randy's computer, his several boxes of warm clothes, and his suitcase on the walkway in front of the darkened bus station.

In minutes Randy's black hair was wet; he hated wearing a hat. The cold water was starting to run down the inside collar of his jacket. Looking around he spotted two landmarks. Across the street one way was a white house with a sign whipping back and forth in the wind, reminding him of an old-time doctor's shingle. Across the other way was a gas station that was open. A scrappy young man walked out to get in his souped-up red truck.

Randy jumped puddles, calling out to him. "Say there, could you give me a lift?" He could see the truck had a good wax job— the rain sat up on the hood in little droplets.

The kid eyed him with a lopsided grin. "Where you headed?"

"I'm looking for Frank's cabin. He said everyone would know what I was talking about. I've got a few packages."

"How much?"

Randy was surprised by the question, but supposed it was fair.

"Ten dollars?"

"Make it twenty. Bring your stuff on over."

Randy placed the computer in the cab. The kid said, "Throw the rest of that stuff in the back."

Less than five minutes later they pulled up by a long driveway. Randy hopped out with his computer. The kid jumped out and set the rest of Randy's things from the truck bed onto the wet grass.

Randy begrudgingly dug the twenty out of his billfold. The kid snatched it. "Name's Joey. You need anything else, just give me a yell."

Joey slid into the driver's seat and stepped on the gas. Water splashed all over Randy and his belongings.

As he watched the taillights disappear down the road, Randy's thoughts were downright nasty. He wondered if his green eyes were glowing in the dark. He felt like a prowling wild animal, angry on a stormy night.

He made five trips up the drive, mumbling all the while. "You bet, Joey, you'll be the first person I'll contact if I need help. Welcome to Squatters Corner, Mr. Tabano. It's a wonderful place. You'll love it. The people are friendly. The scenery is spectacular."

Randy had always had great strength in his upper body. But by then he felt like his hands hung as weights dangling at the end of each arm. It was that feeling of exhaustion again, like he wasn't going to make it from one spot to the next.

He had stood on the little front porch searching for the key that Frank said was so easy to find. Randy hated the thought of stepping into a cold cabin that was seldom used. Because of the dark he'd have to grope his way around until he found a switch. He hoped they were up to date on their electric bill. He placed the key in the lock, and what appeared to him to be a miracle took place. It was warm inside.

Things had been set up on a timer. This cabin was full of surprises. As he closed the door a few lights came on. The fireplace ignited. The radio in the kitchen area came on with soft background music. Randy hoped it was due to technology rather than an old family ghost. He called out to make sure no one was inside.

He moved his few things just inside the door, not wanting to track in mud. Next he removed his wet shoes and jacket.

Immediately, he looked around and found the full bath on the main floor with the thick towels hanging on the racks. It felt good to wipe his face and hair dry. He then went up the stairs, quickly looking into two small bedrooms. Randy was amazed that there was another half-bath, with shower, in the master bedroom.

Opening a closet, he discovered a navy terry-cloth robe. Wrapping himself in it, he tied the belt. He gave a deep sigh; things were getting better. He should have known that Frank would not have built a modest cabin.

After recalling those things he wrote on the tablet:

Friday—arrived evening
Saturday—remember nothing
Sunday—had a visitor

• • •

It had taken a while to figure out how to open the garage door out back. The key to the rusted Jeep had been in the back of the closet in his room, just as Frank had said. On Monday daylight presented a healthier view of Squatters Corner, so he decided to have a look around.

The sign by the crossroads claimed the population was around one hundred. He parked the Jeep in front of the combination bus stop, post office, and grocery. It seemed like a good place to start. This was where the helpful stranger had dropped him off on Friday night.

Next to where he parked was a crossroad. Straight across was the white house he had noticed on Friday; it was a doctor's office. That seemed odd in this lonesome place. There might be a story there. On the other corner was Jo Jo's Pub.

The gas station was across from him. Next to the station was the Laundromat. Stepping inside, he found no collected lint scattered about. No machines out of order. Even the windows were squeaky clean. It left a good impression.

A public phone was outside. There was no phone book, the

same as in big cities. The receiver was dangling loose. Apparently the last user was not satisfied with his call. Randy replaced the phone in its cradle, then picked it up to see if it worked. He was encouraged to hear the steady buzz.

The next window stopped him cold. Was he dreaming? It was a coffee shop and bakery. It seemed out of place in these lonely surroundings. It was decorated with warm browns and gold, creating a decidedly upscale atmosphere, very inviting.

It resembled the one where he and Jill had spent a rainy afternoon in Australia. They had said few words. No words were needed. They were on their honeymoon. It had been fourteen years ago. It had been a wonder that the passion that passed between them as they held hands had not melted the finish on the table. Where had the passion gone? He missed it so desperately. He'd investigate this place another day.

• • •

Back across on the other side he saw the pharmacy.

Krismus Drug Store
Ice Cream Parlour
Gifts and cards
Book exchange
And just about
anything else
your heart desires

He'd browse in there another day, also.

What he'd completed on his book was still in the #10 Vidalia onion box. The paper and other supplies were packed in his Laredo western boots container. He'd worn the boots just for kicks. Jill had given them to him last Christmas because he was always saying that when he grew up he was "gonna be a cowboy." That was before life started going downhill.

It was getting dark. Returning to the cabin, he realized it was time to go to bed. He dreaded it. At least he didn't have to lie there wondering why he didn't have the desire to move closer to Jill. That hurt so. He didn't understand it at all. Maybe his self-esteem was so low that he didn't even have the confidence to love anymore. His love for her remained strong, but he kept his distance. Why? He was so confused. His lack of emotions left him feeling lifeless.

He began to sweat, and that sick feeling started to take over again. "No! This is a new beginning. This is not going to overpower me."

Randy lay on the bed. The moon was shining through the big windows. One thing that surprised him was that for the past two days he'd been so busy investigating new things that he hadn't had as much time to feel despondent.

That bit of encouragement let him drift off to sleep. His last thought was that tomorrow he would try listening to the mountains.

CHAPTER 4

Squatters Corners
Tuesday morning, March 20, 2012

Early Tuesday morning Randy ate a quick breakfast and went out to open the garage again. The snow had melted. Checking the gas gauge he knew he'd have to fill up before returning to the cabin.

Even the desire to look around the outer area was surprising to him. Feeling his heartbeat quicken under his flannel shirt was exciting.

While passing along country roads Randy observed the housing, the colorful birds darting about. He cut back on his speed. To hurry was wrong when taking in such scenery. The snowcapped mountains towered around him.

"Nuts! Forgot the camera," Randy mumbled. "Mustn't make that mistake again." He knew Jill and the kids would want pictures of the cabin and to see what Squatters Corner looked like. He laughed at himself. "I need to get a dog to talk to. If the natives see me riding around talking to myself they'll have me out of here before I've settled in."

With that Randy brought the Jeep to a standstill. Climbing out he took a deep breath, then blew the air slowly out of his mouth. He could truly feel the healing begin. "Come on, God, I'll give you a ride in my chariot."

The road curved to the left after the next stand of trees. He pulled the Jeep over and parked it.

"Good grief! Better keep binoculars with me, too." There was a small lake. At one end were a handful of fancy newly constructed condos. On the hill stood a castle, something that seemed very out of place.

It was huge and gave the impression of being cold and unfriendly. Randy wanted to turn and run back up the road so the trees would hide the monstrosity. He shuddered.

Glancing at his watch he realized it was early, but not that early. Were there living creatures at the castle? It reminded him of a place that would have killer guard dogs.

Then he heard a motor bike. A helmeted person gave a wave as he passed. Randy watched as the biker made his way down the roadway. The rider pulled into a dirt road below where Randy stood. It was then that Randy spotted the half-dozen cottages partly hidden at the base of the hill. Smoke rose from their chimneys to ward off the early morning chill. There was some normalcy in this cluster.

There were definitely some secrets to uncover in this strange place. Who did the large structure belong to? Why had it been built here? He thought there should be gargoyles projecting from the rooftop gutters. It was the type of place that would stir a child to have nightmares.

Randy walked backward all the way to the Jeep. He would go no closer. Turning the Jeep around in the middle of the road, he headed back to civilization.

The return trip was not as cheerful; the emptiness of the road gave him the willies. The beauty had faded with the sun. A strange atmosphere was filling the air, nothing really visible, but it was as if a haze was constructing a wall around him. The Jeep bumped along the road. It seemed as anxious to leave this place as Randy was.

Randy's mind must have remained at the eerie castle. After pulling into town he sat in the stilled Jeep, staring out through the dirty windshield.

• • •

Doc Storey was standing at the file cabinet in his office trying to catch up on old work when he noticed the Jeep pull up. Recognizing it as Frank's, he knew it must be the writer from the city. News traveled fast in a place this small. That was one of the adjustments Doc had learned to make when he had arrived from Missoula six years ago.

He could see the driver through the clear windows of his office. The younger man had broad shoulders and a strong, handsome face. He appeared to be off in a dream. His countenance was lifeless. Doc thought, If this fella can be made to smile, the women in Squatters Corner will be falling over each other for a nod of greeting from him. Heaven help us all if he's unattached.

Doc had a strong feeling that this man needed to make contact with him. Yet the stranger seemed unable to proceed. Maybe a little help was in order. Spotting the weekly paper on the porch, the doctor found his excuse.

Randy watched the door of the white house open. An older man with a full head of white hair stepped out to pick up a rolled newspaper.

Short and stocky, brown-framed round glasses, leisure clothes, and comfortable looking, well-worn hiking boots. Randy was relieved; at least his writer's responses were kicking in. He hadn't realized that he had pulled up in front of the doctor's office. Why? How long had he been here?

With no hesitation Randy climbed out and walked toward the kind-looking man. "Are you the doctor?"

"Yes, I am. Can I be of service to you?"

"Could I come in and talk a bit?"

"Certainly."

The office was spotless, small, and seemed to be sparsely furnished with little equipment. Randy became skeptical. "What kind of a doctor are you?"

Doc smiled. "I'm not a quack. I'm just your old-fashioned general practitioner. The missus and I ran across this town on vacation. We were looking for a place to retire. We fell in love with the area. This house was in disrepair. Not long after it was shipshape my wife died. That was about five years ago.

"After that I decided to open the front rooms as an office. I had a family practice in Missoula. Now I'm like a substation. It saves folks from running into where it's busy and time consuming. I do some things in conjunction with the city doctors. That involves follow-up visits. Saves them a lot of time. Most of them are so backed up with appointments that they appreciate the help. In fact some of them are setting up clinics in surrounding areas to relieve their situations."

A small bird hit the window and tumbled to the ground. Doc shook his head. "Happens every spring. Hopefully he's only stunned, poor thing."

Randy shifted in the chair. Doc continued. "Anything serious, I make sure they head on into the bigger areas. Minor things I can handle. I know how to do it all, and keep up on the latest procedures, just in case. But I prefer to let the younger men handle the tough stuff. A few emergencies have come up. Then I'm glad I'm up to date.

"Every Thursday I'm officially open. Even have a retired nurse who helps out. Usually pretty busy that day."

Randy said, "I'm sorry to have interrupted whatever you were doing. I can make an appointment."

Doc felt that if he permitted this man to walk away it would be a mistake. He had a feeling that his sitting across from him had not been planned and would not be repeated unless a connection was made with this opportunity.

"Say, I'm ready for a cup of tea. Will you join me?" He felt like there was a tiny angel sitting on his shoulder whispering in his ear. "Hang onto him, Doc. He needs you."

Doc got up from the swivel chair and motioned for Randy to follow him. "Let's go to my living quarters in the back. I don't want to work on the file folders this morning. I haven't had a good talk with anybody new in weeks. I'll finish my story, then you can tell me yours.

"If I'm going away any distance I leave a note on the door as to my approximate whereabouts.

"Nurse and I do preschool vaccinations. The kids like my Band-Aids. I use the ones with cartoon characters and crazy sayings."

"I only have plain tea, nothing fancy. If I want to be overpowered by the herbal stuff I go to the tea shop."

"What about the tea room?"

"I'll tell you that another time. Those kids think I'm helping them. What I'm doing is keeping myself going. Sometimes I wonder if I retired too early."

They sipped the hot tea and relaxed. A companionable relationship was beginning to form. "I'm doing everything backward. What is your name?"

"Randy Tabano."

"That sounds familiar. Do you write columns for newspapers?"

"That I do."

"I'll be darned. I've read some of your articles. Now that is exciting, you've perked up my day."

"What is your name, sir?"

"We need to clear that up right away. It's definitely not Sir. I've been called Doc so long I forget that I do have a legal name. Just call me Doc, then you have my full attention. I know, by now you think I'm just some old guy who talks all the time, and most likely spreads everybody's business all over town. Not true. I'm just excited to see a new face. I want you to get to know about me. Then I'd like you to tell me about yourself. I'd like you to feel comfortable and be happy. That doesn't work if you are walking around with your pockets full of secrets. Life isn't worth living unless you have friends, people you can talk to."

Doc kept right on speaking, and Randy couldn't resist laughing at him. Laughing, oh how good that felt.

Randy learned about the doctor's bartering for homegrown veggies, cake, and soup. About how he felt needed, wanted, and part of everything in the community. How happy he was. He mentioned unplanned pregnancies. How he did counseling. As far as he could tell there was no physical abuse in the immediate area. Yes there were some emotional and mental difficulties: he could only go so far with some things, but he had an excellent list of specialists.

The teacups were pushed aside, and Doc looked at Randy square on.

Chapter 5

Squatters Corners
Tuesday afternoon, March 20, 2012

"Well, Mr. Randy Tabano, I'm going to sit here quiet now, and listen to you. I'd like to know who you are." Doc hoped he hadn't shut this young man down. He so wanted him to open up to him.

Randy smiled. "Is it my turn?" Where to begin. Randy scratched his right ear.

"I had been employed by the Coeur d'Alene newspaper since college—on-the-job training. As I developed my writing style I did a lot of freelance work on the side. You know, articles for magazines, and I've been working on a book."

"What type of books do you write?"

"At this point mainstream fiction. I like to throw in some mystery, history, and travel. Haven't settled in on a specific genre."

Reaching in his back pocket Randy withdrew his billfold and opened it to a photo. He sat there a minute gently running his index finger across the woman's face. There was a tenderness in his gesture.

Passing it to Doc he said, "My wife Jill. That's Danny and Trish."

"Does your wife model?"

"No, but she could. She's beautiful, through and through.

"We were just an ordinary family. Then my uncle died. We were shocked to learn that he had numerous stocks and bonds in his safety deposit box. Plus a will that was extremely generous to all of us. He had no family of his own.

"Jill and I talked for days about how to handle the money. Finally, we decided that it was an opportunity that I shouldn't overlook.

"For several years I had talked of wanting to write a novel. I'd actually been working on it, bits at a time. But I'd wanted to concentrate on the book. The inheritance enabled me to step away from my job at the paper, part-time. Frank guaranteed me my full-time position back if I wanted it.

"Life became more like a story than the everyday struggle most people deal with."

Pausing to look out the window, Randy shut his eyes for a few minutes, then he continued.

"So, we reorganized our home life to accommodate my schedule. It worked out surprisingly well. I put in a lot of hours, Monday through Friday. The weekends were for family, yard work, and an occasional social outing.

"Jill continued with her different volunteer endeavors."

Doc put his hand up to make Randy stop. "No day off for true rest and pulling back?"

"It seemed like we were more rushed than we'd ever been. We never missed any of the kids' activities that we should attend. Maybe we tried too hard to be 'the perfect parents.'"

Randy sucked in his breath and sat still. "Come to think of it, maybe I have just spoken the secret words. It hadn't entered my mind before. Maybe because I worked at home I thought we should appear to be the ideal family to our neighbors and friends. I honestly don't know why I was feeling so confused. That was when things began to feel like they were collapsing. I had always been able to do everything on my own. I was so proud of that. Then when my uncle gave me a big lift, I felt guilty, like I was coasting along on someone else's hard work. It seemed wrong. Like I was a little rich boy who had everything handed to him."

Randy bowed his head and began to cry. "I've never even thought of things this way before. I'm sorry."

Doc couldn't keep his eyes dry either. "See, that's what friends are for.

"It's the same as watching a mother when she starts a job outside of the home. She thinks she must do everything, the husband, the kids, meals, the laundry, any obligations she previously had. Does she, or we, think people will think less of us if the transition doesn't run smoothly? Are vultures waiting to see if we falter? Strange what we put ourselves through.

"You and Jill ever get away by yourselves?"

"I was pushing hard on the book and we didn't think about it. One day just worked its way into the next. All of a sudden it dawned on me. My priorities were self-centered. I didn't do it purposely. I honestly don't think we were aware of it.

"Maybe this is my slap in the face. A hard way to learn a lesson.

"Because I was known within the publishing circles, I was lucky. My first book was snatched up. Now I'm on my second. It isn't that simple. There's a lot of complicated hard work that went into it. It's a lengthy, difficult process."

Doc studied Randy carefully as he spoke, "So Frank loaned you his cabin."

"He thought it would bring me back among the living. Jill and I decided it would be worth a try. I'm a mess, and it doesn't go away just because I want to fix it." Randy rubbed his forehead with his finger tips.

"So, financially we're okay. I adore my wife and kids. We have friends and are busy like most people our age.

"I don't feel sick. I just feel . . . sick. A clinical statement. No appetite, no passion, I've lost interest in everything around me. I have no drive. I pick up my pencil but it sits idle in my hand. I feel like a walking dead man." Randy slouched in the chair.

"I'm aware of depression and stress problems. We lost some good people at the paper with those maladies. But this seems ridiculous. There's no reason for such debilitation. Yet, I'm lost. I feel like I'm standing on the sidelines watching the world play its game without me. Sometimes I don't have enough energy to box with my own shadow.

"If a simple question is asked, I can't seem to make a decision, come up with an answer. My brain doesn't always function."

They had walked back to the office, but it hadn't registered with Randy until Doc reached in one of his desk drawers. Pulling out a small dictionary he thumbed through the pages. "Shadow-box: to make the motion of attack and defense, as in boxing. As a training or conditioning procedure. To avoid or evade direct or decisive action."

Doc turned the book toward Randy, who read the same words aloud, then sat there thinking.

Doc opened by saying. "You took your first action when you decided to try and solve the problem instead of drowning in it."

Randy cocked his head and sat up straight.

Doc pointed his finger at him and said, "Now, we'll start the cure for your dilemma."

"I guess if I talk more I'll be repeating myself. But I do feel like an empty shell. Like my soul has hibernated in a hidden corner. I have no energy, yet, I'm restless."

He sat back looking tired and drawn.

Doc said, "One question, do you have a cell phone here with you?"

"No, I left it home. The only hookup with the outside is a radio."

"Good. A few more general facts. Our little community has some eccentrics. Lots of good folks, and a scattering of rotten seeds. The beauty tramples the bad ones, and grows wild flowers in their place. Wrap love around you like outstretched arms. You can't blot out the foolishness in the world. It's here too, but not as obvious as some places. Use your brain less and your eyes and heart more. You may think you are in heaven, if you think along those lines.

"Me, I'm inclined to think heaven is here on earth. That each person has to produce their own heaven, or is it haven. No matter where you are there are those who will disrupt your quest. Some will be vile and threatening. Others will be a nuisance and slow you down. Each of these is valuable in helping you. They teach a patience, understanding, and grit.

"In a few minutes one of my regular patients will be coming through the door. You visit with him. I'm going to step into my private office and write down some important information for you."

 CHAPTER 6

Squatters Corners
Tuesday afternoon, March 20, 2012

Randy watched the little boy pull into the driveway. He made a perfect twist around and the dust flew into the air. Grinning, he parked his scooter by the steps. The door was whisked open, but closed with great care. The attitude became subdued. Obviously he had been taught proprieties.

The scooter looked old and homemade. The boy was wearing overalls and a red-and-white plaid shirt that didn't appear to be store-bought. His scuffed-up cowboy boots looked like a treasure that would be difficult to remove from a boy at bedtime. His bowl-type haircut topped him off perfectly. He was so full of life that Randy held his palm up to catch a piece of it to carry in his pocket for luck.

"Hi, is that your Jeep?"

"It goes with the cabin I'm using. My name is Randy." He stuck out his hand to shake the boy's.

The handshake was returned. "I'm Billy. I've got an allergy to dogs 'n' cats and stuff. Doc gives me a shot the middle of each month. I have to pull my shorts down a little—'cause that's where I get the poke. Did you ever have to do that in a doctor's office?"

Billy didn't stop talking. "I don't mind the shot but that shorts business is, well you know." He made a face.

Randy gave him a light slap on the shoulder. "I sure do, pal."

They both started laughing.

"How long you figure on staying?"

"I'm not sure."

"It's a nice place, you'll like it. You got kids?"

"A boy and a girl. They're a little older than you."

"They comin' here to live?"

"No, I'm not going to be here that long."

Doc came back into the room. "Well, Billy, did you tell Mr. Tabano about The Corners?"

Randy looked at the doctor. "The Corners?"

Billy smiled, "Squatters Corner only has two of 'em so that's what most of us call it."

"Billy, you can go on in. I'll be right with you."

Doc turned back to Randy. "Read the instructions in this envelope. Before you do anything you need to go to the pharmacy. My first order is to get yourself a root beer float. The girl who works at the fountain refuses to wait on anyone unless they smile."

"Will they accept a credit card for prescriptions? I haven't had time to get my money straightened around. I assume there is a bank in the nearest town."

"You won't need your card to fill this. Come back a week from today. I'll need to see if this works for you."

"How much do I owe you?"

"I don't deal with credit cards. First visit is free. Next time the price goes up."

Randy rose from the chair but paused. "Do you think Billy would like to join me?"

Doc responded, "Give me a minute to make a phone call." He stepped through the door again to the private part of the house.

Randy was thinking about poor Billy waiting in one of the examining rooms. His shorts were ready for the quick unmasking. By now he probably thought neither Doc nor Randy was being very kind to make him wait so long.

Doc returned. "It's a go. It will be a rare treat. Then he must go home immediately. He has to change for afternoon kindergarten."

As the doctor ushered them out the door he smiled. Randy realized that the man had just given him his first dose of medicine in the form of a small boy who would generously share his enthusiasm for life itself.

Billy took hold of Randy's hand. When they entered the drug store, a tiny bell jingled above the door. Billy's voice rang out loud and clear. "Hey Merry!"

"Hey! It's my buddy, Billy."

Randy could hear someone moving through the rows of shelves but still saw no one.

He and Billy seated themselves at the counter. Out of the corner of his eye Randy caught sight of movement.

A pair of shoulders and a small head with short curly brown hair and brown eyes passed speedily by the end of the counter. The pretty young woman hopped up and was standing directly in front of him.

He opened his mouth but no words popped out.

By this time the young lady and Billy were in stitches.

Billy blurted out, "Isn't Merry special? She says she's a 'Little Person.' I think she's just the right size."

Randy pointed at her. "You're the Merry who set up the welcome at the cabin."

"That's me."

"Well I'd like to shake your hand. I can't tell you how pleased I was. You're a gem of a girl."

"Mr. Krismus built me sort of a runway back here to make me look taller. If I'm not at the level people expect me to be they feel awkward when placing their orders. I'm sort of in show biz."

A fine smile spread across Randy's face. He knew he'd be waited on by this little charmer.

"We are needing a couple of root beer floats, doctor's orders."

"Comin' up, Mr. . . . What's your name?"

When introductions were completed Randy knew that Merry had taken the last name of the owners. He and Billy sipped that good foamy root beer through the straws and dug around in the bubbles with the long-handled spoon, fishing out globs of ice cream. Merry Krismus. What else? She looked to be in her late twenties, early thirties.

"So, are you from here Merry?"

"No. I lived in Birmingham, Alabama, with people like myself. Don't honestly know my background. It was hard to get good-paying work. But us Little People stayed together and pooled the money we made. We could take care of our needs.

"I was doing my regular cleaning in the church one day when the minister asked me to come into the office. He explained that he knew an older couple in a tiny town in Montana. They owned a drug store and felt they had reached a point where they needed a full-time helper. They couldn't pay very much but were hoping they could provide a home for a reliable person.

"The minister said if I'd like to give it a try the church would pay my bus fare. I threw my few belongings in a satchel and I came from Alabama with a . . ." She plunked on an imaginary banjo. "Here I've been ever since."

When Randy and Billy got to the bottom of the soda glass they had a contest to see who could make the loudest slurping noise. Afterward Billy hurried on home.

After paying the bill Randy sat there running some facts through his mind. He was thinking of the weaving in and out of the businesses, characters, and area surrounding this little village. Who knew what might wash down from the mountain streams?

The exciting creation of fiction could use it all. There were microscopic pieces of everyday life that could slide subtly and smoothly into stories. If used in completely different settings and incidents the facts and names were often unrecognizable, so not harmful in any way. Randy enjoyed the powerful search for stirring emotions. He found that the words that pull the reader into the story are magnets.

He was excited. His writing brain was working once again.

He glanced up to find Merry studying him. "Welcome to The Corners, Mr. Tabano."

He reached in his jacket pocket to remove the doctor's envelope. He'd better read the instructions inside to see what he'd prescribed.

CHAPTER 7

Squatters Corners
Tuesday evening, March 20, 2012

The bell over the door in the drug store announced another customer. In a sing-song voice that sounded familiar came some words. "Is little Merry here? I can't see her."

Randy frowned. He felt a small soft hand pat his hand several times. In a quiet voice Merry said, "It's okay, Mr. Tabano. I'm used to it. It's no problem."

Then the voice became agitated. "I need help here. Cut my finger. There's blood and I want you to get me some gauze and tape and help me wrap it up."

Merry sighed and walked away. After helping Joey and ringing up the bill but receiving no thank you, she asked, "You want to buy a St. Patrick's Day card Joey? They're half price."

"That's a dumb question. I don't know any saints."

The bell vibrated for several seconds after the door was slammed shut.

Randy breathed in and out slowly several times.

"Folks around here get used to each other's ways after while. Some are good, some bad. Might as well accept them. They won't change. Makes it easier on yourself."

"Do you have any supplies for a writer in your store, or do I have to drive into the city?"

"Probably not much for serious writing. But when you have time you should give us a thorough look. If I told you everything on the shelves, I'd sound like that guy Bubba in *Forrest Gump* who went on for days, listing the ways to fix shrimp. We do have movie houses in the nearby towns. There are talkies, and in color, too." With that she hurried away to answer the phone, grinning from ear to ear.

Could you possibly leave this store without a smile on your face?

• • •

When Randy arrived home it dawned on him that he'd only glanced at Doc's note enough to know that he didn't have to pick up a prescription. He made himself comfortable in the old easy chair and studied the list carefully. It insisted he leave the Jeep parked and walk everywhere, unless traveling a long distance was absolutely necessary. None of this "weather permitting" foolishness. If he didn't have the right outdoor gear, Doc could round some up for him to use temporarily.

He felt Doc's presence and could have sworn that it was his voice that uttered the words written on the paper.

> *Walk until you begin to feel tired, then turn and start home. Study everything that surrounds you. Eat healthy meals. Relax. Catch a short nap once in a while. It worked for Winston Churchill.*

> *When you do go off, leave a note in the cabin telling of your tentative plans, when you left, and some idea of your return time. That way if you get lost we'll have an idea of*

which way to head out. Someone will notice when there are no lights in the cabin. Preferably head home long before dark. The mountains at night aren't a good place for the inexperienced.

You're on your own. But don't hesitate to reach out for a hand if you need assistance.

It sounds strange to make a claim that The Corners is entertaining, but it's true. Meet the people.

You had some questions. You'll have more by next Monday. Make a list. We'll get to them.

Work on your book if you feel like it. Do not isolate yourself in the cabin. Cabin fever is not good for folks. That would only make things worse.

Freedom, discovery, investigation. Don't drink the coffee at Jo Jo's. It'll rot your stomach lining. If you like to bake and you ever make chocolate chip cookies, I am to be notified pronto.

He listed his emergency number.

Randy fell asleep in the old chair with a smile on his face.

CHAPTER 8

Squatters Corners
Wednesday, March 21, 2012

Dear Ones,

I miss you with all my heart. I need to mention that right off, because if I tell you first about the last four days you won't believe that I miss you at all.

With that Randy proceeded to tell every detail since his arrival, except for one. He couldn't bring himself to mention the young woman he'd seen on Sunday. Nor could he pinpoint the reason for his reluctance. He set the completed letter beside his billfold. Next time out he'd mail it at Bishop's.

It was then that it hit him. Oh, how good it would be to hear from back home. He did miss them, but he needed to get his bearings.

Even if he did step backward sometimes, each forward movement was a tremendous gain. A moment of feeling unsteady had him grasping for the countertop. Taking a deep breath, he looked out the window at the clouds.

As he stepped outside, the clouds parted and the sun warmed his face. He caught a movement at the edge of the trees. It was a deer. He headed that way, slipping into his jacket as he went.

He wouldn't go far today and would stay close to the edge of the trees. Maybe he'd go into the woods tomorrow. If he kept the cabin or the town within his sight he wouldn't get lost. Randy could picture the headlines. NEWCOMER LOSES WAY IN WOODS—SEARCH BEGINS.

He'd not seen the deer again. After walking for miles he deliberately fell to the ground and rolled down the hill like a small child.

Randy came to a sitting position and laughed out loud. He wished he had a singing voice; he'd fill the mountains with an operatic number. The woods would ring and echoes would bounce back through the air.

Standing up again he spread his arms out like wings. Would the populace wonder whether he had found freedom, or dub him Mad Man of the Mountain? No matter. This was the reason he was here.

The following day he went to the window at the back of Bishop's grocery that acted as the post office. He established his temporary residency and mailed his letter.

Each day his bravery increased. The woods were never-ending. Randy followed the stream and spotted a pheasant.

He was sloshing down a nearby country road, heading home so that he wouldn't get caught in the rain, when he spotted the young woman again. They waved at each other.

She was on horseback. Her horsemanship was apparent. She had on high boots, tight pants, and a long-sleeved shirt. Her hair was tied back out of the way and she wore a helmet.

She was concentrating on the horse's performance as she worked on different maneuvers. She smiled as if satisfied, then rode toward him.

Pulling up beside him she asked, "So how's it going, Mr. Tabano?"

"Good. How do you know me?"

"I only know of you, sir. Hang in there."

"That's not fair. Tell me your name."

"Shawn Winslow."

It was surprising he caught it; she stated it in a rush while turning the horse and riding away. Maybe lengthy conversations were not her thing. The niggling consequence was the less he knew about her the more intriguing she became. That, however, was not why he was here. The situation provoked an uneasiness within him.

He hadn't worked on the book, but he had unpacked and organized his material. He had come up with a good-sized folding table that he found in the shed out back, so things were spread out and ready.

Before the week was out he received mail. Jill wrote about how busy she had been. There were the meetings at the church, the phone ringing all the time, someone wanting her to organize a supper at school honoring the teachers' aides. And the monthly book club.

She admitted it was the usual routine but said she felt there was a gap in her life. She wondered if each reached out toward the other they would feel their fingers touching. Randy's arm automatically stretched toward home. A wave of loneliness swept over him.

The kids had included a note.

Dad,
Mom says you are out in the boonies. Send pictures.
School is going okay.
Trish and Danny

• • •

On Sunday Randy walked to the church. Arriving minutes before the service was to begin, he slipped into the back pew. Everyone sat quietly.

Randy waited and wondered. Maybe this was it; folks just gathered to release their cares, and to meditate.

The side door squeaked a little as it was opened with great effort. A man with tufts of white hair shuffled to the pulpit. His suit hung loosely from his shoulders, as if he had lost considerable weight lately. Had he not been well? He was stooped over, with tiny glasses that continued to slip to the end of his nose. He needed his large feet to hold him steady. Randy felt sorry for him;he appeared ancient.

The man chuckled while looking over the familiar faces. When his gaze reached Randy he paused. "Welcome, young man."

No one turned to stare or embarrass him. When the pastor began to speak Randy sat at attention. Age may have weakened the man's body but not his voice. That was deep and crisp and reminded Randy of the actor Richard Burton. It wasn't that he was loud, but his words were spoken with a clarity that reverberated throughout the sanctuary.

He did not quote scripture. He did not use notes. He spoke of the problems in the world today. His mind was sharp.

He told the people that the happenings around the world were but repeats of the past. He shared stories of how folks had been frightened throughout the centuries.

The pastor assured his flock that God was still watching out for them. He discussed how they could understand better by looking at things from all sides, encouraging them to keep the faith and do their best.

Randy was mesmerized. He was one of the last to leave the church.

"Reverend, thank you."

"Are you joining our little community, Mr. Tabano?"

"Just for a short while. You helped me a lot today. You know my name."

The pastor smiled. "Yes. I'm glad you joined us this morning. You see, I know why people come to the mountains. I'd like to share some thoughts with you. Let go. Let go. Allow the mountains to come to you. We talk to God about our troubles. He already knows what they are. But we spend little time listening to him. Be still and listen. He will help you. Listen. Often it takes time even for him to come up with some helpful ideas. We have to learn to be patient.

"Will you stop by and see me one of these days? I live around the corner. My wife died years ago. There's a couple of young ladies who see that I eat properly and they keep me in clean dishes and laundry. I enjoy conversing with new folks. I need to hurry on. Sunday dinner awaits in the crock-pot."

Randy stepped away and wished him a good-bye. He had caught a glimpse of Shawn and she had smiled. But everyone had left the parking lot as he began walking home. As he moved along the side of the road he was thinking about the pastor. Maybe another story.

 CHAPTER 9

Squatters Corners
Late March–early April, 2012

Monday morning, the twenty-sixth, Randy kept his appointment at Doc's.

"So, how did my prescriptions work?"

"Quite well. I've had some moments, but generally things are improving. I've worked on my story from time to time."

"You have also walked, rolled down foothills, and tried to fly."

They both laughed heartily.

"No secrets around here."

"Very few."

Randy paused a minute. "Several times I was sure someone was observing me. I mean, way out in the woods. And a couple of times when I was at my writing desk. I'd swear there was a movement somewhere. Searching with the binoculars turned up nothing. Am I imagining something?"

"That's Old Will. He showed up here before I did. A harmless vagrant. No one knows his real name or where he stays. He poaches a little. Those who have laying hens miss an egg once in a while, and on rare occasions a chicken.

"I hike a lot myself. You and I will probably run into each other. Then I can tell you more of the history of these people. I have to make some house calls this morning. I'll be around next Monday about this time. If you feel you need to come in, do.

"I want you to meet my secretary sometime. She's my granddaughter, does filing and book-work. She works two days at the grocery in town, and one day for me. The balance of her time she devotes to her newly acquired husband who runs the gas station. She came out here to visit me."

• • •

On his way by the post office Randy dropped a note to his agent explaining the new return address.

He spent the afternoon on his book, and made plans to go to the pub for supper.

Jo Jo's was dark inside, so it took a few minutes for his eyes to adjust. There was a man who looked about his age sitting by a side window. He motioned that Randy could join him.

When Randy reached the table the man stood. They shook hands and exchanged names.

Roy Sheldon's menu suggestion was chili and homemade French bread.

Talk flowed easily. "I fly up to see my dad a lot, he's getting on in years. Sometimes my wife Sally joins me. If you ever need a lawyer, my office is in Great Falls. I'm probably passing out more information than you care to hear. We all heard that you were on your way, for a little peace and quiet. I hope you enjoy your stay."

Randy mentioned that he was writing a novel, and that so far he was finding the townspeople friendly.

"My dad is retired from the training stable up the way. They have a small landing strip they let me use. Very kind of them. It was originally developed for the Winslows. The owners of the stable still call on him if a horse comes in that seems unmanageable. I guess you never lose the touch."

"Say, since you're connected in some way, with the stable . . ." Randy stopped, not sure what he wanted to say.

Roy smiled. "You've seen the girl."

Randy felt foolish.

"I know, you're married but you'd like to know something about her. Don't be embarrassed. I'm married, too, yet I'm curious. She does draw attention. I don't think anyone knows much. She steers away from most, but she is a beauty. No getting around that. If anyone does know her secret, he isn't telling. Dad claims she's a lovely person. Then he clams up."

It made for a pleasant evening and a nice change in routine. As they shook hands upon leaving Roy said, "If I come this way, it's on Monday. I'm a creature of habit. If I am here I'm at Jo Jo's eating the special. Dad plays cards with the boys that night, then he and I spend the balance of the evening together. They break up around nine. So if you're looking for company you know where to find me."

"Great. I'll look forward to seeing you again."'

More people to write home about tomorrow. For the first time in months his desire to have Jill beside him was strong. It was comforting. It was as it should be.

• • •

On Tuesday when he went to place his letter to home on the counter in the post office he was surprised to discover his box contained a piece of mail. He would savor the unknown sender until he reached home.

Sitting on the deck to open it, he found it to be a printed invitation to attend an event at the Winslow Manor House on April 14th. He was more confused than anything.

As he tried to figure out this development, he heard someone crossing the creek-bed. He looked up to see Shawn, astride a horse, looking down at him. He was puzzled after what Roy had told him.

Standing up, Randy handed her the invitation. "Could you explain this to me?"

She didn't even glance at the wording, but handed it back as if it had been written with a poison pen.

"Go, but be forewarned, be careful. This woman is a very strange person. She means no good."

The girl was shaking as if someone had struck her. Whirling the horse around she headed across the creek and off into the woods.

Randy felt a chill. How odd. She had acted as if she might talk to him, and then she rode as if to escape a private demon.

Sometimes this place seemed like Utopia. Other times there seemed to be an undercurrent waiting to drag him down. A quiet threat.

• • •

He didn't care to walk in the mountains Wednesday. This might be a day to stop by the pastor's house. Randy yearned for company. Maybe he could treat the man to a visit at the fancy coffee shop, tea shop, bakery, or whatever it was. He must discard this unexplainable feeling of despair. Unfortunately, the pastor was under the weather and asked if Randy could come by another time.

Would the girl return? What had upset her?

He tossed the envelope in a basket on the countertop and decided to forget it. He didn't want to deal with it at this point.

• • •

Running into the doctor later on Thursday on a mountain trail was uplifting. "Doc, you've been here awhile. Do you still find it as beautiful as I do, being a newcomer?"

"I find it fascinating. Every day is a new day. I'm at peace. Winters are tough, but I'm not planning on moving on. Did you ever make out that list of questions?"

"Let me think. Let's start with Billy and his family."

Randy could see that Doc was putting things in order by the look on his face. They headed for some good-sized rocks and sat down.

"Billy is six. His mom didn't enroll him in kindergarten until this year because she wanted to give him every advantage possible. Her husband had an alcohol problem. One day he just drove away. He was in enough trouble along the way that they followed his trail easily enough. She filed for divorce. No one knows or cares where he is now.

"Babs moved in with her dad, who has a small farm at the edge of town. She's paid all the bills her ex left behind. Works at the school as an aide, and once in a while she'll help out at Jo Jo's on a weekend, but only during the day.

"That lady does not trust men, the bum saw to that. You'll spot her easy, she's a pretty little blonde, looks like a Barbie doll. One nice lady. I hope someone comes along and convinces her that there are some good men in the world."

Doc looked down at the town in the distance. "She and her dad have done a fine job with the boy. I'm trusting that you will not repeat the information I share with you. I'm just trying to stabilize your thoughts so you know something about these people."

They were up and walking again when Randy spoke of the pastor. "He says the town is going to change."

"I think that's due to Harris Coffee and Tea. I agree with him. That's a neat tale but I'm going to hold that for another time.

"I want to touch on something else. If you end up with time on your hands, there are a couple of offerings.

"The paper in Livingston sends a special edition to our fair city once a week. They would no doubt be impressed with you as a contributor. Also there's an old-fashioned hardware store on the same block, if you wanted to do something completely different. They always need part-time help. Just a thought."

Randy smiled. Different wasn't a descriptive word. To set him loose in a hardware store wouldn't be a good plan. Experience as a store clerk could be disastrous.

Randy and Jill were keeping the mail service busy with their weekly letters. Jill passed on information about the kids' activities. Randy wrote poems describing the creatures in the woods and tried to draw pencil sketches of the mountain ranges.

• • •

It rained hard all day Sunday, the first of April. Randy had his story rolling and, other than drinking coffee, never left the bedroom. When he had to turn on the light, he realized he was still in his pajamas and famished. Stopping his work for the night, he fixed a sandwich.

He thumbed through the few pages of Livingston's *Mountain Review*. Not earth-shaking, but with the lift of new blood it might have possibilities. Randy did like the name of the paper. He wondered if he could provide photos of local interests from a newcomer's view. Maybe he could show them some from his previous travels, as well.

He put the idea aside for now. He was sure it would be freelance work.

• • •

On Monday he walked to Jo Jo's hoping Roy would appear. Randy was half-finished with his chili when Roy slid into the other side of the booth. After they greeted each other and Roy had placed his order, Randy laid the invitation on the table. "Do you know anything about this?"

Roy didn't pick it up. He seemed to know its content. At least his reaction wasn't the same as the girl's.

Roy gave him a sarcastic smile. "Go, it's a learning experience. A must for a man like yourself who knows how to observe a situation. It's at the eccentric mansion you saw out away from town."

"Why was it sent so far in advance?"

With that Roy laughed out loud.

"Because, my man, you are the honored guest. It's not really a request for your company, but a command. Others will receive theirs in time. It's not as important that they attend."

Randy rubbed his forehead with his fingers.

"I'll make it simple. The hostess likes younger men and you are new in town. When I started coming up here I got the same treatment. She was quite put out when I was not smitten with her charms."

"I don't participate in games like that. I'm a happily married man."

"That is even more enticing. She will be more diligent. If I get an invitation, I'll have Sally join me."

"I'm going to see if Jill and the kids will come up over spring break. It's that week. I'll take her, she enjoys social things."

With that remark Roy slapped his hand on the table and motioned for the proprietor to bring him a second beer.

"This calls for a celebration. Does your wife really look like the picture you carry in your billfold?"

"Better."

Roy put his hand on Randy's shoulder. "Don't tell anyone that you are planning to have her accompany you to this open house. My friend, it will be a night to remember."

All of a sudden the color drained out of Randy's face. "Spring break is next week."

Roy handed Randy the cell phone from his pocket. "Call now."

Randy couldn't stop apologizing to Jill on the phone. "I can't even think of a decent excuse, Jill. I've had it on my mind to suggest an open invitation. I am so sorry. Will you forgive me?'

"I'll not only forgive you, you bum. We will be there."

Randy talked to Trish and Danny, too. The excitement in their voices brought tears to his eyes.

Roy put his hand on Randy's shoulder. "It's okay man, I understand."

One thing Randy felt he and Jill needed to discuss was the once-a-week letters. It had turned into a lot of repeats, on both sides. They had each lost the novelty of the exchange. They were becoming empty. Was this separation producing a negative effect, not the positive spark they had hoped for?

• • •

Heading back home, Randy stepped to the side of the road. With his horn blowing and traveling at a high speed, Joey waved as he passed.

Peering up ahead, Randy saw a figure dart across the road. Joey veered off the road toward the man. Just as quickly, the truck returned to the pavement and was gone.

Randy hurried on to see if the fellow was okay. He figured it was Old Will. But he had disappeared without a trace.

Joey was the one person that Randy didn't trust. He seemed to get his kicks from hassling and hustling people. He'd charge twenty dollars to drive someone a quarter of a mile or so, then deliberately drench him with cold slushy water. Randy's list of people he didn't like was short, but Joey was persistently trying to hold his place as top dog.

CHAPTER 10

Squatters Corners
Early April, 2012

It was the first week of April, and Randy wondered if he should return home with his family after their visit. In deep thought as he walked in the woods, he heard a distant hello. The briskness of the morning air above the tree line was refreshing. But he would be happy to share his inner thoughts with Doc and get his opinion.

Randy spoke of feeling like a prisoner in his own mind. How sometimes everything seemed to turn gray and there was no movement, like the weight of silence was unbearable. And how it poisoned his imagination.

Doc laughed at him. "Randy, you think too much. You waste time trying to figure out how life works. It can't be done, you know. Try to relax and let life happen.

There was not a moment's hesitation in Doc's answer. "Have you ever gone to the doctor and he prescribed an antibiotic? On the label it states: Take until gone. If you don't follow instructions the illness may return. Often times you feel even worse. You get my drift?

"Being here may not be the answer, but you are considerably better than the first time I laid eyes on you. My advice would be to give it more time.

"You've been here just short of three weeks. Something that works into your system slowly doesn't disappear in a poof because your mind has decided you've had a change of attitude.

"Makes me think of the schizophrenic. After being on medication for awhile he feels normal, so he quits taking the pills. Pretty soon everything goes haywire. Back to the doctor, back on the pills. It happens again and again. It's terrible for the family. If the patient remains on the medication, he can sometimes lead a good life. If not, it's not uncommon for things to get steadily worse. I'm getting morbid here. Do you understand what I'm getting at?"

"When my family arrives I want you to meet them, Doc. They are worth knowing. They're special, and fun to be around."

Released from the seriousness of the discussion, they climbed higher for the sheer joy of it.

"You promised you'd tell me about the tea room."

"Harris Coffee and Tea. The Harrises were born just up the way. Grew up, got married and ended up in Australia. I don't know that part of the story. Roscoe's father died and left him the farm.

"He didn't want to sell out, but wanted to come back and modernize it. He claims Susie agreed to move if she could pick up a challenge of her own. She wanted to bring her favorite coffee shop with her. She'd worked there for several years and knew the ropes. He's in his early forties; she's around thirty-five, no young ones."

Doc asked to stop and rest by some wild berry bushes.

"Before I head home I'll pick some of these. I've got a container in my knapsack. They make great pancakes.

"The coffee shop is unbelievable. When you walk through our

little town and come upon it, it makes you stop in your tracks. Every single thing she makes is delicious. It's amazing the amount of business she generates.

"More and more people are making distance drives to check it out. She's beginning to advertise in travel magazines. People who are vacationing put it on their list of stops. She says she's going to put Squatters Corner on the map.

"You been there yet?"

"I've been holding off, afraid it would become a regular habit. Think I'll save that to share with Jill. I did offer to treat the pastor when I stopped by, but he wasn't feeling up to par that day."

Doc rose. Rummaging through his sack he produced two containers. "Thought I might run into you. Those who help pick get to join me for breakfast."

Raising his voice he shouted, "Hear that, Will? Pancakes tomorrow. I'll leave you a couple of hot ones on the shelf by the window."

Without blinking an eye, he said, "It's the one thing we didn't change when we fixed the house. Women used to have a shelf outside their kitchen window for cooling things."

"One more quick question, Doc. How did Squatters Corner get its name?'

"What I heard was, years ago someone arrived here and they felt like the squatters who had worked their way out west. To be honest, I never thought about the name of the place."

• • •

Randy's most recent letter home had been a long one. He wanted the family to be even more familiar with the folks from Squatters

Corner. He hoped that their visit would feel to him like putting his arms in the sleeves of a warm jacket on a cold day.

The following morning, after he returned from Doc's pancake breakfast, Randy sat on the steps of the deck. He felt panicky. How could this happen? Was he worried about his family, joining him for a week?

This made no sense to him. There was that sinking feeling in his stomach again. He gripped the edge of the wooden steps. It had to pass. He was mad at himself. Why couldn't he control something like this? That was the problem, not being in charge of himself. He must concentrate on the doctor's advice. It will take time. Think of all the good things that were happening. Do not get bogged down with the moments of insecurity.

It was then that he heard the sound of horse's hooves. Shawn observed him with a worried look. "Something's wrong."

Trying to push his feelings aside he said, "How could it be?"

She dismounted, dropping the reins. The horse began to graze.

Sitting beside him she pried his one hand free and just held on as if comforting a dear friend. His other hand went up to cover his mouth; tears filled his eyes, and he sighed. Neither of them spoke. An understanding passed through their clasped hands.

After a few minutes Shawn began to talk. Her voice was soft, soothing, calming. "I have been where you are. It is a lonely and frightening place. Never think you will be left there alone. Always see my hand reaching for you. I will not let you go. You have too much to do. Don't let go. Feel for the rungs of the ladder. Climb. I will help. Your life is full of good things. You are needed and wanted. Hang on." She squeezed his hand firmly.

Randy relaxed and closed his eyes. When he opened them, Shawn was smiling.

"You see, if someone is there with you, it's not as bad."

She released his hand.

Then, as if she was just a neighbor passing by, she began to chat about simple things. "You should plant some flowers when the weather warms. I must go. I work with horses from the training stable. I'll stop again sometime for just a minute."

She hopped up, gathered the reins, and mounted the horse in swift easy movements. They each waved.

Not an alluring mermaid. She was a guardian angel. Randy looked skyward and smiled at someone whom he felt had smiled down on him. Someone who had provided an understanding hand on his and helped him hold back those walls that were threatening to move closer.

Was there someone up there pulling strings, helping him by providing kind hearts and hands that were guiding his path? He wasn't sure. One thing he did know: his spirit was floating higher on the horizon.

CHAPTER 11

Squatters Corners
Early April 2012

Tuesday morning, the third of April, Randy woke up feeling nauseous. Would he feel better if he stayed in bed? No, get up and ignore it, go about your business. A man shouldn't feel this way just because his family is visiting. Anxiety was all it was. He did come up with a faint smile because he knew he wasn't pregnant! Oh, poor Jill, two times she had gone through those morning bouts.

He swung his feet to the side of the bed and jumped up, nearly falling from unsteadiness. To heck with this routine. Throwing on his sweats, he made his way downstairs. Putting on some old shoes, he sat down for a minute. He got up slowly and went to the kitchen. A banana, an apple, two pieces of bread spread with peanut butter and jam went into a brown lunch sack. He swallowed a glass of orange juice before heading out the door.

He moved slowly, letting the fresh air do its work. He needed to get away from the cabin. One thing at a time. Everything would be okay. He mumbled under his breath, "It will work, won't it, God? We'll make it work."

The next day Randy hired Merry to put the cabin in order. He'd been carelessly collecting dust and a few other things. He wanted the place to be in tip-top shape for his family's arrival. They must like the cabin as much as he did.

Shawn had stopped by upon hearing that Randy's family would be coming. She invited them to come to the stable for a tour and promised a ride into the mountains that would not soon be forgotten.

There was no school on Friday. Randy knew they would arrive on Saturday, but he didn't know what time of day. He sat on the porch with the anticipation of a kid waiting for his folks to bring home a new bike.

• • •

He spotted the car when it turned the corner by the church. At that point he realized how anxious he was to see them.

He was afraid he was going to lose control and burst into tears. He tried to stand up nonchalantly as they came closer. Later he would discover that his plan hadn't worked. Trish and Danny reported at supper that he had jumped up like a jack-in-the-box.

The kids were out of the car almost before it had come to a complete stop. They hugged their dad several times, then ran into the house to look around and check out their bedrooms.

Jill got out slowly. Then she and Randy were running toward one another. They held each other tightly; neither wanted to break the connection. Then they both spoke at the same time. "It's been so long. I've missed you. I think about you all the time." Then they were laughing, holding hands, and walking toward the cabin. They decided unpacking could wait.

Trish and Danny came running outside. "Oh, Dad, it's so cool."

Doc was on his daily hike, hidden by the trees. After witnessing the arrival he decided he would present himself at a different time. They needed this time for themselves.

Later, after the kids were asleep, Randy and Jill sat up in bed talking. The free-flowing feelings that had blossomed during the family's arrival continued. They each thrilled to the fact that the depth of their love was still intact.

• • •

Randy had suggested they bring church clothes, one dressy outfit for Jill, and rough-and-tumble for everyday.

First there was their Easter basket custom: Randy's contained some new disks and other small supplies for his writing. There also were a goodly number of fancy chocolate bunnies that Jill had made. He had temporarily forgotten about her delicious hand-dipped chocolates, and all those molds stored in the attic. So much talent. Naturally she had brought things for the children.

Randy looked forlorn. He hadn't got her anything. "Honey, I forgot."

"Being here is more than enough, Ran. You are my Easter bunny." She gave him a sly wink.

Church was grand. A woman with a beautiful voice had come to sing some familiar songs. Everyone in the pews sang out in response. The welcome Jill and the kids received made Randy exceptionally proud.

• • •

Randy had written about Roy in his letters home. He and Jill decided to eat at Jo Jo's on Monday, hoping that Roy might be there. The kids had begged to have hotdogs at the cabin. They seemed to love spending time there. As Jill and Randy walked to town Randy suggested that Jill go on ahead, as he had to stop at the post office and mail some material to his publisher.

"As soon as you're through the door look off to your right. That's where we usually sit."

Jill's first thought was that the lights were very dim, and she had to get acclimated to the surroundings. She looked off to the right when she entered and saw a couple with their heads together in quiet conversation.

Someone had taken over the men's favorite spot, but the gentleman rose. She could see he was tall and carried himself well. He came toward her with his hand extended. "You must be Jill. You look just like the picture Randy carries."

Jill stood there blinking her eyes with a confused look on her face. "Roy?"

"Didn't he mention . . . ?"

"No."

She reached for his hand and shook it with firmness.

"Then our friendship draws no line on color. It is genuine. I'm pleased."

When Randy walked to the table Roy introduced him to Sally. Jo Jo's special was ordered all around. Randy and Jill would pick up the other two for the Winslows' open house on Saturday.

CHAPTER 12

Squatters Corners
Mid-April, 2012

Tuesday morning there were footsteps on the porch of the cabin and an excited knock at the door. Jill looked at Randy, who shrugged his shoulders. "Come on, you guys, obviously someone's at the door." Trish jumped up. When she opened the door she was greeted by a big smile on a small boy.

"Hi! I'm Billy. You and your brother want to look for deer tracks along the creek?"

"Come on in and grab a donut. We'll get our jackets. I'm Trish and that's . . ."

"Danny, I know. I been excited about your comin'."

• • •

Billy went home about eleven. At lunch Danny asked, "Dad, how come you didn't tell us you had a cat in the shed?"

"Because, as far as I know, I don't have one."

Trish spoke with impatience. "You've got a mother tiger cat, and four kittens born within the last few days. There's a comfortable nest area made with old blankets. A makeshift litter box, and a bag of cat food. Why didn't you give her some milk and water?"

Randy looked bewildered, but before he could make a sound

Danny piped up again. "The old man wondered if we knew when a kitten was big enough to leave its mother."

"What old man?"

"Billy knew him, called him Will."

Randy was astonished. "I have a cat family I know nothing about, and Old Will was in my shed. Is this a joke?"

"Really, Dad, how could we make up something like that?"

Looking at Jill, Randy said, "Let's gather some supplies and go check things out."

The little family was residing in a tidy corner of the shed. Randy kept shaking his head. "Gather round and I'll tell you what little I know about Old Will."

• • •

On the evening of April 14th the kids babysat with the kitten family until dark, and the grown-ups went to the party.

It wasn't just any party: it was an extravaganza at the Winslows', in the mansion, by invitation only. When they came over the top of the hill Randy slowed down and pulled over to the side of the road. Roy had seen the spectacle before. The other three sat there speechless. Finally, Sally said, "What on earth?"

"Amazing, isn't it?" commented Roy. "You really ain't seen nothin' yet."

There were thousands of lights. Surprisingly, it didn't appear gaudy. It shimmered like a fairy-tale castle.

As they drew near they could see cars parked everywhere. Most of them looked expensive. Where could they hide an ordinary family vehicle? A man stepped in front of their car. He informed them that he would have someone take care of it. They were to enter through the large double front doors.

The two women made no attempt to hide their surprise with the surroundings. A maid ushered them into a powder room. At the moment they were the only occupants. They said nothing, but their eyes exchanged messages. "For heaven's sakes don't laugh."

"No," said Sally. "We mustn't make fools of ourselves."

The room remained empty, then Sally said, "Is this for real? I've got to see the rest of this charade."

The men waited in the hallway for their wives. A woman glided toward them. Roy greeted her. "Mrs. Winslow."

"Good evening, Roy."

Randy detected a cutting edge to her voice. It reminded him of Shawn's warning: this was dangerous territory. She linked arms with Randy and her voice turned sensuous. "I finally have the privilege of meeting Randy Tabano, our resident writer."

The men heard the powder room door open and close. They turned and in unison said, "Our wives."

The woman at Randy's side became rigid. He was positive that if she had been a dog the hair rising on the back of her neck would have been visible. Her look was not disguised. Her eyes pierced the wives with dozens of arrows.

The muscles in Mrs. Winslow's jaw tightened. Without releasing Randy's arm, she turned with him in tow. Her voice was like syrup. "Come, I'll introduce you to some people you need to know."

Roy made his arms available. "Ladies, join me."

There was an older man making his way across the room.

He appeared cordial and was greeting guests as he went. His manners seemed impeccable.

Roy whispered a warning, "Ladies stick together: You are about to be hit upon." Leveling his voice he said, "Mr. Winslow, another superfluous affair."

The man covered his annoyance with Roy's choice of words by turning to the two stunning women whom Roy had been escorting. He made a slight bow. "Ladies." With that Roy also bowed to the women, turning his back on their host.

"If you will excuse us, we'll traverse the rooms and sample the elegant delicacies." They moved into the pulsating throng, leaving the handsome Mr. Winslow with disapproval in his eyes as his countenance changed completely. Fortunately, another guest asked him a question at that moment. He turned and smiled, becoming the gracious host once again.

Roy despised this man and his wife. Each had tried to lure him into their bed. He shuddered with disgust. His appetite had vanished. They circulated through the rooms and the crowd. He so wanted to get his wife and friends out of this lair. He motioned to Randy when he spotted him, and the message was loud and clear.

Randy explained to Mr. and Mrs. Winslow that one of the help had relayed a message that there was an emergency at the cabin. This excuse was not accepted hospitably, but with numerous guests showing concern for Randy, the hosts could only graciously extend an invitation that they return at a more convenient time.

The car was brought around. When they reached the top of the hill again, Randy did a quick turn around and shut off the motor. The lights did not represent a fairy castle but a menagerie.

Roy finally spoke. "You have to observe the program in full to appreciate the lesson." Randy turned the car around and headed home. Each knew there was no emergency but that it was a polite way to leave an atmosphere that was not comfortable. An evening that would not be forgotten.

CHAPTER 13

Squatters Corners
Wednesday, April 11, 2012

On the Wednesday before the party, Randy had woken at dawn. He left a note on the counter letting Jill and the kids know he'd gone for a walk. He'd had to get away by himself; he was feeling unsteady again. When he got high enough that the woods covered his existence he leaned against a tree. "Please, God, not now. Don't let me throw a monkey wrench into this time of being together. We need this time, at least I do. I guess I made the mistake of thinking that because they were here I would feel fine. I have been doing so well. Please help me. Please." It made Randy think maybe he should consider Doc's suggestion of a low-dose medication to ease him toward recovery. But no, he'd continue fighting that.

By the time he'd got back to the cabin the tension he'd been feeling had let up. The kids were eating breakfast. Jill brought coffee to him on the deck. She quietly asked, "You okay sweetheart?"

"Getting there. Sometimes I expect miracles."

"I see great improvement. Relax, the miracle is taking place, just not as fast as you'd like." She turned to him and smiled.

• • •

They had a full day planned.

Randy rounded up the family and they drove to the stable area where Roy parked his small plane. When they arrived Roy was going over the checklist of his Cessna 172 while Sally waited in the cockpit. He motioned for Randy and the family to come over by the white-and-blue plane. Randy introduced the kids to the young couple.

"You kids like to know a few facts about this beauty?"

"You bet," answered a quartet of voices. "We all would."

"Then gather 'round. Four hours in the air is its endurance. It carries enough fuel to travel 400 miles. Horsepower max 160. It can go about 125 to 130 miles in an hour."

Danny had almost climbed on Sally's lap trying to get a look at the instruments.

"For safety's sake I took additional flying instructions because I knew I'd need to do occasional night flying and flying in the mountains."

Danny asked, "You ever get scared because something went wrong?"

"Yep. There was an electrical short and it caused the cockpit to fill with smoke. That's what the lessons are for. You must have automatic and instant reflexes to solve emergency problems.

"You know, you are safer flying than in a car, but you can't pull over to the side of the road in an airplane. Flying is unforgiving. You have to have respect for every aspect. A small mistake can be corrected with experience. There is no room for pilot ignorance. Sometime in the future I'll take you up."

Danny shook his head in wonder. "Wow! That will be great!"

Shawn, waiting nearby, made a statement. "I hope the plane doesn't overshadow our next adventure."

Randy said, "Never fear, it will just be different."

Shawn had promised a special horse ride through the area.

● ● ●

Shawn did some short safety lessons before heading out and repeated warnings as they rode, since they were beginning riders.

Riding horseback through the mountains was exhilarating. Shawn warned them all, again, to watch for coyote traps.

"Your horse will look wherever you look. If you are checking a new trail, so will he. If your horse stepped into a trap, it could be devastating for horse and rider.

"You are in charge. Your horses are counting on your leadership." Four riders listened carefully to her instructions.

While they were riding, they heard a friendly shout from just above the trail. Randy introduced his family to Doc with great pride.

After entertaining Danny and Trish and completely charming Jill, Doc said, "Well, I'd better let you get on with your ride. Say, I've got an idea. How would you kids like to accompany me into one of the bigger towns tomorrow? I need to go in and pick up some supplies. We could look around and probably stop at the ice cream shop."

Two voices answered, "Yes!"

"Would you object if I included Billy?"

Trish said, "It would be twice as much fun." Danny seconded the motion.

"I'll be by midmorning."

Randy held his horse back as the rest of them continued up the path.

"Doc, why would you . . . ?" The look on Doc's face plainly said, "Don't ask a foolish question."

"Thanks Doc."

As they progressed Shawn suggested they ride in silence. "Just look and listen."

The wind through the trees was musical. They stopped to watch a small herd of deer. There was a sound like a larger animal crashing through the brush that spooked the horses a bit but they quieted down when they followed Shawn's lead.

When they finished the ride and the horses were brushed and put away, the Tabanos couldn't come up with enough words to thank Shawn for the opportunity.

As they started toward their car, Trish turned and ran back to give Shawn a quick hug. Trish's face was flushed with the combination of mountain air and riding. "It was so cool. I wish I knew more about horses." With that she ran back to catch up with her family.

Shawn remained in the same spot. Her body wouldn't budge. She was trying to recall. Had anyone ever hugged her? Her eyes stung from trying to hold back tears.

So that's what it's like to be part of a real family. She stepped into an empty stall and let the tears flow.

CHAPTER 14

Squatters Corners
Mid-April, 2012

On Thursday Doc and his young guests had had fun scouring the area and filling up on ice cream. Jill and Randy spent quiet time celebrating being husband and wife, taking long walks, and sitting side by side on the steps of the deck overlooking the stream.

Jill sat with her head nestled against Randy's shoulder. "There must be a name for such a day as this. I cannot lay claim to it. Special moments." She sighed. "One of life's treasures. I give up. Everyone needs a day like this. I love you Randy." She turned to kiss him.

That's when Doc's car turned into the drive. Three heads were hanging out the windows yelling, "Oh no. Call the police. Do something quick." Even Doc was laughing.

Later that afternoon Randy and Danny walked to town to pick up more milk and cat food. "Why can't we ride in the Jeep, Dad?"

"Doc says walking is required whenever possible." As they neared the school they were startled to see a parade passing them. There were a couple of pickup trucks. Someone was playing a tambourine and blowing a whistle to set a beat. The women in the trucks all laughed and waved.

Danny looked at his dad.

"You got me."

• • •

Jill and Trish were sitting on the floor of the cabin laughing when they heard the commotion. The banging on the door brought them to their feet.

"Hello in there! The ladies of Squatters Corner have come to welcome you. We bring lemonade and cookies and cheer to your door."

As the door opened the women became silent and stared in amazement. The two females on the inside of the cabin looked like they had been painted in chocolate speckles. The taller of the two spoke.

"We were starting to try and make the boys their favorite chocolate dessert and something has already gone terribly wrong."

Laughter spread like the common cold. Before they could get it stopped, everyone was holding her sides and begging for relief.

Merry pushed her way inside. "And to think I bothered to clean this place up so it would be in good shape for your visit." She rolled up her sleeves. "Well, one more time won't hurt."

Father and son had been goofing off; when they returned all was back to normal, except that every time mother and daughter looked at each other they giggled.

Leftover lemonade was served with supper and delicious cookies from the neighbor ladies for dessert.

When the kids headed up to bed, Jill settled in the crook of Randy's arm. She looked up at him, nothing needed to be said.

• • •

Friday Jill had taken off in the car giving the excuse that she wanted to spend some time by herself. She was gone for hours.

Randy was becoming concerned. When she returned she brought a fancy dessert from Harris's.

Then it had been Saturday. The day of the Winslows' party. The week had gone by fast.

• • •

Sunday, the fifteenth, was when Jill and the kids left for home. Each member of the family was quiet. Not one of them wanted this time to end. No one could come up with the right words. Finally the car doors needed to be closed. No smiles were visible.

Randy waved for the last time when they turned the corner. Was this decision good or bad? He looked at the mountains. He had still not heard them speak. Maybe he needed to listen with more intent.

He was exhausted from the busy week, but his bloodstream was pulsing with joy and happiness. Number one goal: continue to feel well so he and his family could be together.

CHAPTER 15

Squatters Corners
Mid-April, 2012

After the family left, Randy worked hard on his story. He took frequent walks and an occasional drive in the countryside.

A note arrived from Mrs. Winslow. Not any suggestive words, but the indication was pretty clear. She would love to have him stop by any time. Her husband was away a lot on business. The country was so boring, and she'd welcome company.

Randy was walking out of the grocery one day carrying a small sack to replenish his supply cupboard. Billy raced up on his scooter.

"Randy, how are the kittens?"

"Doin' fine, my friend. I think Old Will sneaks in and helps me look after them."

"My school is having a fair April twenty-seventh. That's a Friday. A cake walk and all that stuff. Will you come? Our band is going to play for the first time. Practice sounds awful, but teacher says that by next week we'll be okay."

"I just might show up," he said with a wink.

"I'll watch for you, since you don't know your way around the school, or many of the people. I don't want you to be alone or get lost."

• • •

On Monday Randy headed for Jo Jo's. Roy had flown in again and was seated with his father Logan. The weekly card game had been called off. Randy was glad to finally meet the older man. They stayed well into the evening. Logan was full of information about the folks who populated the area.

Randy told Roy about his latest mailing from Mrs. Winslow. "What's with her?"

"Let me tell you some of the secrets of the castle. Dad will fill in anything I leave out.

"They say if you ever go there when there is not a social event underway, it's spooky. There's a very cold atmosphere, like nothing is alive."

Randy nodded. "I thought there was an undercurrent transmitted through Mr. Winslow's handshake. Almost like an electrical jolt. I felt less apprehensive when he moved on."

"You see, they fool around, but not with each other. They each crave younger blood. You are new and that in itself appeals to her. You have landed in her back yard.

"By all reports, he not only chases beautiful women but also enjoys the rare company of men. I find him revolting."

Roy got the attention of the waitress and indicated he'd like a cup of coffee. The other two let the girl know that they were all set.

"Mrs. Winslow was after me for awhile. I didn't respond and she was furious. I guess she wanted to check out the dark side of life. She sent a few imaginative notes to my wife. I had already detailed the situation to her, so Sally and I ignored it. I have passed from enticing to invisible.

"Surprisingly, sometimes she gets what she wants. Her facial expression doesn't give away what she's thinking. She takes what she wants and leaves destruction behind. It's like a feeding frenzy.

"People who have lived their lives here avoid any contact. Part of the 'growing-up story' to their children is a warning against both of them. Of course, some young people don't listen. The challenge is tempting. They usually leave town after any involvement. Both of them contaminate life."

Putting cream and sugar in his coffee, Roy continued. "Their money is what keeps things moving here in Squatters Corner. So there you have it. I think of her as 'The Dragon Lady.'

"Her composure disgusts you once you are on to the game. I can't imagine why any man would want to climb in bed with her. Each of them leaves me with a chill. Her sexual involvement has nothing to do with love. If she thought anyone felt sorry for her, she would be infuriated. She can talk to you without blinking an eye and say the right things, but if you watch her body language, it sends out some sickening messages. If you can see past the mask, you see the sadness.

"It boils down to the fact that I don't like them and obviously neither do you." With that, he raised his cup in a toasting gesture.

"What upsets me most is they ruin some innocent and beautiful lives. End of lesson."

They sat quietly for a few minutes.

Randy said, "Since we're talking about odd folks, what about that Joey character?"

Logan spoke up. "I got this one. No one knows about Joey's beginning. He arrived here as a teenager. Lived with his uncle, about five miles out of town, on a run-down farm. Don't think the boy finished school. The town has been too lenient with him and accepted his behavior. One of the ways he entertains himself is by screeching through the parking lot of the church during Sunday service. Kicks up loose stones, sometimes you can hear him laugh.

"His uncle died a couple of years ago. No other relatives, so he left the place to Joey. I hear there was also some money tucked away in the bank. First thing Joey did was buy that truck. Gotta admit we are all rather envious of it."

The old man cleared his throat, then continued. "He installed a powerful sound system in the house. If you drive by at night the place is dark, but the music is enough to blast you off the road. Don't think folks would mind so much if it was pretty sounds. But it's dreadful stuff. Thing is he don't do anything to cause serious trouble, just an annoying individual. What he does with the balance of his time, no one knows."

Shrugging his shoulders, he went on. "Maybe he watches TV. They have seen him at that little mall in Livingston playing video games. Not a friend. Even the useless types don't seem to want to hang out with him."

Getting up, Roy said, "I've got to get to bed. I'm flying out early in the morning. A big case coming up. I won't be back for quite a while."

CHAPTER 16

Squatters Corners
Late April–early May, 2012

The letters traveled back and forth between Randy and Jill, but not as often. Randy had put one of her letters in his writing files. Whether or not he could use it to enhance a story in the future he didn't know. The potential was great, but the means he wasn't sure of. He was using a cardboard box that originally held a holiday turkey for a temporary file cabinet.

Jill had told of something she'd seen on the news. A lady was talking about quilts. It seems she had purchased one in the South. The woman who had made it was a descendant of slaves.

The quilts were coded messages hung on clotheslines. The message was contained in the design. A duck pattern: Follow the ducks in the spring when they fly north. They will know where the water is. One represented a bear's paw: Follow the bear tracks through the mountains. They will know the trails.

There were others but she couldn't remember them. It was a sad part of our country's history.

• • •

The days were passing quickly for Randy.

As he walked up the sidewalk to the school fair he was thinking about Billy. Maybe Billy's grandpa would be at this community affair. He must be a nice old gent. Randy hoped to get an opportunity to meet him.

He heard some sniffling; looking around, he spied Billy sitting on some side steps. Sitting down beside him he asked, "What's the matter, pal?"

"I can't show you around my school."

"Why's that?"

"My mom says to stay away from you."

Randy's face turned pale. Had his friendship for this young boy been misinterpreted?

"You know the game we play? The one where you say, 'You're a lot of trouble to me, kid,' and I say things like 'My grandpa calls me wiggle britches' or 'My grandpa calls me scalawag'?"

"Yes."

"Mom says I am bothering you and pestering you and I shouldn't do that. So I'm not supposed to hang around with you any more."

Randy breathed a sigh of relief. "I believe this is a misunderstanding. Is your mom here?"

"Yes, she's working in the room where they have the cake walk."

"Show me where she is and we'll see if we can't straighten this out." Randy reached for Billy's hand to help him up.

Billy would not have had to point out his mom; Randy spotted her instantly. Doc's description was right on the button.

When they reached her, Randy asked, "Could you and I step into the hall for a second? I fear that you have misunderstood something. I'd like to put it right."

"You, I take it, are Mr. Tabano."

"Yes, ma'am."

"Billy, you help with the cakes for a minute."

As they walked down to the end of the hall, Randy explained. "First off, I'm Randy, and I believe you are called Babs. I was not feeling well when I arrived in town so I stopped to see Doc. He introduced me to your son. It was the best medicine he could have prescribed.

"As you well know, he's one fine little fella. He and I joke around. I don't want to lose his friendship. My wife and kids think he's super." He looked Babs straight in the eyes. "I would hope that you understand, and that you and he would be my, and my family's, friends. He has promised to show me his school. Is that okay with you?"

"I appreciate your coming to me, Mr. Tabano-Randy. Carry on." Accompanying that was a glorious smile.

As Randy and Billy toured the rooms, the mothers who were volunteering paused. The women peered past customers to get a look at the man and the boy. The two were having a fine time exploring posted crayon pictures and attendance charts.

"Come on Randy, my grandpa is out here. He's running the horseshoe contest. He's county champ." Together they pushed the bar that opened the heavy door. "Gramps, this is Mr. Tabano." The two men shook hands and conversed.

"He's a rascal, isn't he?"

"That he is, sir."

Randy and Billy worked their way back to where the music was playing for the cake walk. As they walked into the room the music stopped. "Joey, you win. Pick a cake."

He chose the best-looking one. Picking it up carelessly, he juggled it in the air like it was a living thing gone completely out of control. He hesitated, then deliberately flipped it upside down. Frosting and cake were smeared all over the floor.

Joey let go of a high-pitched laugh and with a cocky walk left the room. No one uttered a word. Babs grabbed some paper toweling and began to clean up the mess.

"Gee, Mom, you worked hard on that cake. Said you wanted it to be the nicest one here."

Randy bent down. "Let me help."

Babs looked up at him. "I seem to be destined to clean up messes others make." Their eyes met. She turned quickly. "Let's get the music going."

Randy stood. "Gotta go, Billy. Thanks for inviting me. Nice to meet your family."

He was glad it was cool outside. Walking home cleared his head. "Boy, I'm glad I love my wife. There are a couple of women in this town who could make a man unfaithful if he had a shaky marriage."

• • •

It was May 1st. Randy was about to leave for a walk. When he opened the cabin door he heard a noise, sort of a swish. He looked on the outside of the door and discovered a small basket hanging from the knob.

It was still very early. His eyes scanned the area. Who could have placed it there? Then he saw the horse come charging out of the trees and the rider giving him a big, wide enthusiastic wave.

Inside the basket was a bunch of wildflowers, a carefully

wrapped muffin, and a short note.

> *May Day is when you secretly place a surprise on the door of a good friend.*

Randy chuckled to himself. This silly place left nothing to one's imagination. It was like a fairyland with gumdrop houses. He went back inside to place the flowers in a juice glass filled with water. The basket he put on the stairs. He'd use it to hold his pencils. He devoured the muffin before his feet were off the porch.

Which way today? It was time to follow the road away from town to discover what surprises were hidden along the way. He had driven the road before but not walked it for any distance.

His mind was on his book as he tramped along. He was pleased with the way the story was developing, but right about now it needed some firecrackers.

Would hissing, coughing, smoke, and steam be sufficient? Something was drastically wrong with Joey's truck as it passed. He was glad the boy didn't acknowledge his presence. The look of frustration on Joey's face was enough to scare a black bear. The truck obviously had a major problem, and Joey didn't take to that.

Why did he think of him as a boy? He was a disturbed young man.

There was a mound of large boulders near the road. Randy hastened toward them, seating himself. Here it comes again, that dizzy feeling.

It happened seldom lately, but when it did it still put him in a panic. Things were going well. That's the part he didn't understand.

Randy had to admit that whenever Joey came within sight he seemed to come unglued. Why? Since he had nothing to do with Joey, why shouldn't he be able to let it pass as soon as Joey was out of sight? But the feeling would linger and pulsate.

• • •

A few days later, when Randy and Merry were sitting on the bench in front of the pharmacy, he confessed to her his uneasiness when Joey was around.

For once Merry was serious. "I feel very sorry for him. He has no one. He's a sad case."

"You're showing concern."

"Because there is concern. I fear that the cauldron will boil over one day. It's been bubbling a long time. Someone will get burned beyond recognition."

Randy looked at her.

She said, "Let's talk of something else."

Randy observed, once again, a deeply caring individual.

He jumped up. "I'll treat you to a single-dip, French Silk, waffle cone." That was worth a big smile.

CHAPTER 17

Squatters Corners
May 2012

There were signs of an early spring. If Randy was out and about Shawn would often stop. She'd hop down from her horse, holding the reins, and walk beside him. They talked of cabbages and kings and many other things, but very seldom spoke of anything personal.

Then one bright afternoon she topped the hill near the cabin at high speed riding a different horse. She jumped off, almost stumbling. He started to reach for her to prevent an injury. She appeared ready to rush into his arms. They stopped abruptly. She was crying uncontrollably. He reached for her hands, and they lowered themselves to the steps.

"Tell me."

"The horse I have been working with for so long, my favorite, she's dead."

Randy had put a clean white hanky in his pocket that morning. He handed it to her and released her hands. She cried for a long time. She slowed down, but then started hiccupping. Tears turned to light laughter.

"Explain."

"I knew the owner would eventually come for her, but he

seemed to be in no hurry. She had become—my temporary family. I loved her deeply. I could talk to her and she acted like she understood. She loved me in return, I know she did."

He reached for her hands again. He wanted to embrace her and kiss away the tears. Each of them knew, yet they knew it was impossible.

Shawn began to share in detail what had happened. "She had colic. A horse's intestines are one hundred feet long; the membrane is thin. There was a blockage. We gave her the medications prescribed for that. We kept her on her feet and kept her moving. That's the procedure. Her stomach was gurgling, skin color was good, gums had not turned blue, her eyes had not begun to turn white.

"Last night when it began to thunder and lightning we moved her inside. We put her in the end stall where you can see down both aisles of the barn. Then we brought the older horses in. She stuck her head out into the aisle on the one side and the horses did the same. She turned around and repeated the gesture on the other side. I should have recognized the farewell. She seemed to enjoy our working with her."

Shawn's voice turned to a wail. "I should have known. I should have stayed with her.

"This morning she was dead in her stall. The vet said her intestines were punctured. It would be like if your appendix ruptured, filling your body with infection."

Shawn looked like her heart had been torn out.

"When the men came to take her away in the truck my boss said I was to get on another horse and ride out.

"Do you suppose she knew how much I loved her?"

Randy was trying to keep his own emotions intact. Finally he said, "I'm sure she did, Shawn."

They sat side by side without a word. After a while she stood. "I'm sorry. This has been very hard for me. Thanks for helping."

Randy assisted her in her remount and she rode away slowly.

• • •

Two days later, Randy was again working on his computer. He glanced up. Not able to figure out exactly what he was witnessing, he picked up his binoculars and adjusted them.

Two women were trekking the meadow on the opposite side of the creek. They resembled a wagon train heading west.

They had an overloaded push cart. Visible were a small table, fold-up stools, plus several woven baskets. There were some sticks of wood that looked like they would unfold into something if you knew the secret word. On top sat a white wicker chair with a bright multicolored pillow.

They were struggling and laughing at the same time. Accompanying them was a black-and-white setter.

Randy watched as they created their special spot. It was one of those rare spring days when it's warmer than it's supposed to be. Some wildflowers were popping up and covered the meadow with a colorful carpet.

The sticks were portable easels. There was a pot of flowers placed upon the table. The dog lay in the shadow of the creative construction.

The older woman had her hair pulled back in a loose bun. She had on a long full skirt and smock. She wore long dangling earrings. A straw hat assisted her in evading the sun. The other woman appeared younger. She had chosen a long skirt that was more appropriate for her slender body. She wore a fitted bodice. Topping her head was a colossal hat decorated with fresh flowers.

Randy had never seen such an uncommon spectacle. He could stand it no longer. He ran down the stairs, across the deck and lawn, and jumped over the creek. He bowed and scraped with great exaggeration. "Ladies, welcome to my sanctuary." The older woman looked to be in her late fifties. She had a pretty face and eyes that radiated patience, understanding, and kindness. His instant reaction was a desire for her friendship.

"I have watched you construct your house with no walls. Fascinating."

The younger person began to giggle. Coyly, she tilted her head so he could see her face. Randy stared in disbelief. "Shawn?"

All three laughed and Randy began to regain his senses. "I can't believe this."

"I was so distraught that my boss suggested a week off. So I am spending time with Miss Lydia and we are catching up on our projects. She is teaching me to paint."

"Well, I am pleased to meet Miss Lydia, and the same goes for you, Miss Shawn."

Miss Lydia had been observing this reception carefully. She smiled and spoke, "Suppose you were to return to your writing and let us get on with our work. Then you could rejoin us for a picnic lunch."

"I'll do it."

Randy turned. As he walked away he was considering his good fortune. Words like *beauty, pleasure, people, mountains,* and *stream* painted a natural picture. In addition, there was concentration, satisfaction to the mind. Oh, what this place had to offer! It made his heart feel like it would burst with happiness. Could he have this and his wonderful family, too? It seemed like too much to ask.

"Enjoy it while you can. Write. Fill yourself with this segment of your life."

He raised his arms to the sky. Then he realized he must look like a referee signaling a touchdown. Laughing, he once again jumped the creek in celebration.

Could he incorporate such an incident in his story? It would be far-fetched. No one would believe a word of it.

At lunch they sipped coffee as they finished their cream cake. Some picnic. Miss Lydia sat in the wicker chair.

Randy snapped his fingers. "I thought of something. Saturday, May 19th, there's going to be an English tea at Harris's. The owner has an out-of-town guest, from England, I can't recall his name. He came up with this idea. Would you lovely ladies be my guests?"

They looked at each other. Shawn's eyes sparkled. Miss Lydia replied, "We'd be delighted." Randy offered to pick them up but they insisted on meeting him at the tea room.

"Can I help you pack up and get back to—wherever you came from?"

"No, the light is still good. We are a sturdy and organized troupe. We'll see you next week."

CHAPTER 18

Squatters Corners
Saturday, May 19, 2012

Randy parked the Jeep in front of the sign that announced an English tea was being served.

He had picked out khaki pants and a brown-and-white striped dress shirt, no tie, and he'd left the collar open. With his brown belt and loafers he felt adequately attired. But when he spotted the women coming toward him he suddenly hoped he would not embarrass them.

Miss Lydia and Shawn were in their finery. They were a sight to behold. They wore long dresses, hats, and fancy shoes. The outfits were finished with white gloves, and each carried a parasol. They presented a bewitching pair.

Randy wasn't sure if men attended such an affair. When he had called about reservations for three, and specified a table in the front window, the proprietress had sounded delighted.

Mrs. Harris was serving, as was her house guest. He was dressed in black pants with a stiff white shirt and a red cummerbund and bow tie. He also threw in an English accent with his formal explanation of how to properly serve tea.

He showed the trio to the window seat. The guests whispered about his good looks and were curious as to how the Harris's had made his acquaintance. The decision was made to get details at a later date.

Shawn, Miss Lydia, and Randy each bit daintily into tiny cucumber sandwiches. There were a variety of scones and small muffins and numerous other surprises. The other customers enjoying the event were well entertained by the laughter and openness coming from the window seat.

Miss Lydia opened up a bit about herself. She had gone off to art school, then after graduation moved to New York City. She had enjoyed working at a couple of different galleries. She'd sold a few of her paintings for top price.

During those years her parents had passed away. Tired of the big city, she sold the family home, packed up her few belongings, and drove away, having no idea what she was searching for. She ended up here. Loved the peace and quiet. There was money enough to see her through. If she produced a painting that she felt would add to her funds, she'd go back to New York and visit friends, placing her new collection of work in a gallery.

Even Shawn seemed to learn some new facts about Miss Lydia.

As they were leaving, Mrs. Harris rushed over to them. "I couldn't have afforded the advertisement you three provided, in our window. I must do this again sometime. You have made our venture a success."

Turning to the two women Randy stated, "When she sets the date, my dear friends, you mark it on your calendars. Then we shall meet here again." He bowed low and kissed their hands before they once again slipped their gloves on. "A most enjoyable afternoon, indeed, ladies."

It turned out to be a memorable occasion. Although it began as a gesture of thanks for an afternoon picnic in the meadow, it grew into a celebration of genuine friendship among three people.

CHAPTER 19

Squatters Corners
Late May, 2012

Randy paused to read a faded sign newly placed in the window of Krismuses' drug store. It was cockeyed and held in place with wide masking tape.

Don't forget the summer horseshoe
tournaments held in back of the
church on Friday nights.

Billy came running around the corner of the building. "Hey, Randy, you'd like that. Even if you don't want to throw the horseshoes, come watch. Lots of people show up. My mom says it's a gossip gathering. They talk about you if you show up and talk about you if you don't."

"It's time for me to be thinking about going home to my family, Billy."

Billy's smile disappeared. "Oh . . . The weather's been good, and they decided to practice this Sunday after church. First they're going to have a potluck. You could at least see how much fun we have."

"I'll see."

"Hey! What about the mother cat and her kittens?"

"You know, I hadn't thought about that. Do you have any ideas?"

"My mom and I have been talking about me taking one of the kittens. Gramp said he could use the whole lot of them in the barn. We need mousers."

"One is missing, you know."

"Mrs. Gray. I think Old Will took her. He needs a friend. That is the one he always sticks in his jacket pocket while he's setting down fresh water, and keeping their spot cleaned up."

"You and Will see each other often?"

"We run into each other once in a while. He's a nice old man. I'm about the only one he talks to."

• • •

Roy was still tied up with his trial. Randy felt badly that he hadn't said anything to Roy about his own upcoming departure.

Randy hadn't anticipated difficulty in leaving this out-of-the-way place. He was surprised by his reaction. As he began to bring it up in conversation with the people he had become close to, he was equally surprised with the way they were taking it.

He saw Miss Lydia up by Bishop's and hurried that way. They exchanged greetings and she brought up his plans to return home. They began discussing different things in the area that he had missed.

"Say, one place I have been curious about. You know where the road forks; one way you end up at the Winslows', the other winds around to the small houses tucked under the hill?"

"Yes, that's where I live."

"I didn't know that. Does the lake have a name?"

"It's called Landmark Lake. Years back it helped to guide many travelers."

"And the people now?"

"My door is always open to you, Mr. Tabano. Before you leave, invite yourself to visit my humble home."

She left him standing there. Leaving here was getting more difficult by the day.

• • •

The month of May was coming to an end. Randy had purchased his bus ticket. He'd leave on Monday, June 1st. He'd already started packing things he wouldn't be using until he got home.

He was working on his book when he heard someone calling his name. He went down the stairs. Shawn, atop the horse she was working with, was waiting up by the deck. She handed him a brown package.

She didn't seem to have her voice under control. Her words came out in short spurts. "I hear you're heading home. I brought a present for you and Jill and your children, so you won't forget us."

"Should I open it?"

"Please."

The paper and twine came undone easily. It was a wonderful painting of the cabin.

Randy looked up with tears in his eyes. "It's beautiful." He was afraid to say more.

Shawn choked back words that were in her heart. "Thank you for being my friend, Mr. Tabano." She whirled the horse around and rode off.

Randy closed his eyes so he could not watch her trail off in the distance.

• • •

The following day it was dark and the rain was heavy. He had packed his writings. Putting on his rain gear, he headed for the houses under the hill. It was a long walk but he did not know what else he could have done with this day. His thoughts were in turmoil.

He looked the houses over, then headed toward the door of the one that he felt might belong to Miss Lydia.

Randy knocked lightly, and was greeted by her and the English setter. "Welcome." She hung his coat to dry and wiped his boots and placed them on a throw rug, motioning for him to be seated.

They sat studying one another. Finally Randy spoke, "Please, tell me about the people who live in these houses."

Miss Lydia gave him a soft smile. "That is not why you came here."

Randy hung his head. "No, it isn't"

"You wanted to ask me to look after Shawn. I've been doing the best I can for the past few years."

"But I . . ."

"I know, you just wanted to make sure."

His eyes looked around the room: soft colors, pretty pillows, flowers. It was a very cozy atmosphere. Then the fact reached out to him. This was Shawn's safe place. "I have to go."

"I will tell you about these people and introduce you to them when you come back."

Randy started to say something, but she interrupted him. "You will come back, you know."

He slipped into his boots and she held his coat. "Safe journey, Mr. Tabano."

• • •

He was thankful no one came to see him off. He would not have handled it well. He was in much better health. Now if he could just get over the cure. He would need the bus trip and flight home.

The plane out of Billings reminded him of the real world with all the sounds, bustle, and busy routine of things. He hadn't missed it. But it would be great to get home to his family.

CHAPTER 20

Coeur d'Alene
Summer and Fall, 2012

Randy had the taxi driver set his things down in the driveway. Putting his wallet back in his pocket reminded him of something. What a quarter-mile ride and a drenching by the driver had cost him in Squatters Corner.

He had to leave that place behind him. Was it possible? It had worked its way under his skin.

Grabbing a bag, he walked into the kitchen. Trish and Danny were into the milk and the cookie jar. They had just returned from school. Both of them stared at him. He felt out of place in his own home. Not having considered that, he felt awkward.

"Do I still live here?"

With that the after-school snack was forgotten. "Dad! How come you didn't let us know?"

"Thought I'd surprise you."

"Wow! This is great. Are you back for good?"

"You didn't rent out my chair at the table, did you? Where's Mom?"

"It's her turn to work at the photo shop on Wednesday evening."

Randy sat down on the stool by the phone. "She never mentioned working."

Trish smiled. "Jill Tabano is a new woman. You know she's always been well organized and productive. Well, watch out now, buddy-o.

"She's had to be different; she was top dog, not the lady of the house. She's done a great job. You better be proud of her. We're all proud of you. You're a fighter, a winner.

"Come on, Dan, let's help Dad bring his stuff in."

As the cab pulled in, Randy had noticed how well kept the yard was. That must be "Dan's" territory. His wife was working and being a supermom. And Trish was growing up.

Two and a half months; it seemed like a long time. He wasn't the only one who had changed. He wasn't the only one who had given it a best effort to hold things together.

The three of them had Randy's things put back where they used to be in no time. After that they shared cookies and milk and had a crash course in catching up on the home front and The Corners.

• • •

A bit later that evening Randy pulled into the mini-mall and parked in front of the photography shop. A customer had left the store, and Jill had turned her back to work on some shelves.

"Pardon me, miss. If I were to purchase a camera could you give me a loan? I mean, since you're working and all." Jill turned and ran around the counter. Tears ran down her cheeks and she was laughing at the same time. She started kissing him. Then she pulled back and looked at him. Finally she started hugging him.

A man came from the back room carrying a stack of boxes. "I do hope that this is the Mr. Tabano you talk about all the time."

Randy began to laugh. "I was just wondering if she greeted customers this way. If so, no wonder you hired her. Business must have really picked up."

The men shook hands.

"It's quiet tonight, Jill. You two have some catching up to do. Take her to supper, man. There's a romantic Italian restaurant around the corner."

It was a bit early, so the supper crowd hadn't arrived. They each had a glass of wine and sat looking at one another. Jill kept sighing. Randy reached for her hand.

"According to reports by the kids, there have been some changes all around."

"All satisfactory, I hope."

They were finishing the meal when the waiter came by to light the candles. Randy paid the bill and they returned home. Home. Yes, all was satisfactory.

When they reached home, Randy brought out the painting Shawn had done for them. They all agreed it was something they would treasure.

• • •

Before they knew it school was finished, and the kids were into their summer activities. Jill was busy at the store.

Randy finished revising his book in July and was dealing with the publisher. They were setting up a book promotion schedule, with a signing, to be held in early November.

The carefree days passed quickly, and the calendar turned to September.

During October they carved pumpkins as in years past. Jill had picked up a special carving kit at the mall. Danny was turning into quite an artist. They went out twice to buy additional pumpkins. Pumpkins were all over the house spooking out of every window. Danny won a contest at school for his holiday artistry.

It was November when Randy returned home from a tiring trip to the publisher's office in New York City after his many appearances at booksellers. The loyal reading public were happy to meet a new author and have him sign their books. There was something about waiting in line that appealed to them. From Randy's point of view he found it laughable. He often wondered if the average person cared what the story was about or why the author wrote it.

Once in a while there would be someone who really was there about the subject and the process. Someone who sincerely wanted to talk to the writer and know something about him. That did make it worth your while. To those few Randy offered a well-meant smile. This was not his favorite time. He was exhausted. He muttered to himself, "Not good, not good at all. Mustn't let myself get too tired again. Maybe a few days off would be wise."

As he entered the front room of their home, his family was waiting. "Are we having a meeting?"

"You need a change of pace, Ran. We all do. We'd like to go to Squatters Corner for the Christmas break."

Randy slid into an easy chair. A smile began to spread across his face. "Well now, that's an idea to consider. They say there's lots of snow. But maybe Frank and his family are going to use the cabin."

Jill smiled back. "They are flying to Hawaii."

Randy jumped up. "Somewhere I've got Doc's number. I'll call and see if we can make it in during the month of December."

His exuberance was plain when he walked back into the room. "Doc says we're tough. He's sure we can get through. I invited him for Christmas dinner. I hope that's okay."

They were all on their feet dancing around in a circle.

"Doc says he doesn't do the Christmas tree bit but he'll have one cut for us. It will be waiting on the porch."

Oh, the plans, secrets, and surprises that whirled through the household in the next weeks.

Chapter 21

Squatters Corner
Christmas week, 2012

It was dark when they pulled into the drive. As they got closer to the cabin, the porch lit up with tiny Christmas lights. When they opened the door Christmas melodies filled the warm space. The fireplace lit up like the first time, and lights went on in the kitchen.

In the sitting area was a perfectly formed tree. On the kitchen counter were a package of cranberries and a large bag of popped corn. There were four needles, thread, and a pair of scissors.

Randy stepped to the other side of the tree. He was about to turn back and apologize to his family for breaking down when he became aware of soft sobs.

Circling around he rejoined his family. Jill's comment was, "How could you stand it here, Randy? It shakes your emotional stability, it's so comforting."

"At first it does. Then it rebuilds it and makes you strong."

Trish piped up with, "This is not being festive."

Then Danny said two sentences. "I'm hungry. Let's move the stuff in." And in came the boxes, supplies, and wrapped packages.

Danny had made a small carrying sack for Billy to use when he collected things in the woods. Jill had baked fancy holiday cookies for Merry and her family. Trish had carefully wrapped a silver chain with a horse's head for a person she admired. Randy was so moved. Who could ask for a more thoughtful bunch?

The next day they stopped at Krismus's to deliver goodies and hugs. Plus, they thanked the culprit for their welcome. Merry admitted Doc had helped. The two of them had had a hootin' good time, according to Merry.

Merry handed Randy an envelope from Miss Lydia before he left to return to the cabin. Upon opening it at the cabin he felt a sadness. Before he read it aloud he said, "I'm sorry, Trish, You're going to be disappointed."

> *Mr. Tabano,*
>
>   *Shawn and I don't do Christmas. But we are going someplace where it's warm for a week or so. Sorry we'll miss you all.*
>
>   *We'll catch you next time. The happiest of holidays to you and yours. Things are going well.*
>
>   *Miss Lydia*

"Is Miss Lydia the lady who paints, Ran?"

"Yes. You know what we'll do? Tomorrow we'll drive you up so you can see the houses under the hill. There's a safe little box at her house where people leave her notes and things. If we leave your gift for Shawn there, Trish, she will be sure to receive it. I'm sorry, I know you wanted to see her."

All the while he was speaking, he was thanking Miss Lydia in his mind. The message at the end meant a lot to him.

• • •

Christmas dinner was terrific. Doc brought each family member a token gift. For Randy he had found a pocket dictionary and had underlined "shadow boxing."

Each apologized for not bringing him a present. Doc sat back and folded his hands over his full stomach. Looking from one to another he smiled with satisfaction. "You have given me the most precious gift of all, a family."

With that he rose to go home. At the door he asked Randy how he was doing.

Randy replied, "Thanks to you, quite well."

"You have no one to thank but yourself. Keep up the good work. Merry Christmas."

• • •

Spending time trudging in the woods to see how winter was treating the landscape and spending time with Billy chasing footprints in the snow was fun for all.

But the best part was the time spent together. No rush, no places to rush off to. Four people getting to know each other, again cherishing each moment. Priceless.

Then it was time to drive the snow-covered roads back to civilization.

CHAPTER 22

Coeur d'Alene
Winter, 2013

Randy and his family had thrived in Montana over the holidays. He had been disappointed that the good feeling had dissipated so soon.

All fronts promised a discouraging winter in Idaho. Snow, sleet, and ice closed many airports, and left people stranded. It would be a fine time to be a bear and hibernate.

Randy had written to a friend trying to relieve his own feeling of being in the doldrums.

He often felt like the world was getting too heavy for him to deal with.

• • •

One day he stopped by the church they had been attending in Coeur d'Alene. The pastor encouraged him to pray more. Randy did not feel like his heart was lightened by the suggestion. It made the burdens of life seem heavier.

He often walked the streets through the slush, hunched over and cold. Wandering, looking for a cheerful note to raise his hopes. Thank goodness for the kids' school activities. It was the invigorating feeling he gained from watching them participate and cheering them on that kept him going.

Knowing that spring would follow helped immensely. He had never been bothered by the dreary winter months before. He and Jill went to the movies, and they gathered with friends. Somehow it presented itself as mundane.

"Come on, old boy, get your act together." He tried getting back some spirit by enrolling in a fitness center. After two weeks he went back to struggling through the messy sidewalks in the park a few blocks from the house.

One day as he was walking, the clouds parted and Old Man Sun shone down upon his face. Looking up with a smile back he exclaimed, "Where have you been? I've needed you. About time you showed up. You've been hiding on me.

"Thanks, up there, whoever runs the show. Don't know as I've been praying. But I've been talking to you a lot, lately. Thanks for showing me your happy face."

Randy turned from the busier walkways and found his favorite bench. It was more isolated than the others. The shrubbery that kept it partly hidden was bare, but it still had the effect of a secret hideaway.

The bench was cold but the wind had blown the fluffy snow off.

"Maybe the clouds have been hiding your kind face. I feel your presence. Are you real or imaginary? Could you help me to understand things? I know that I feel more confident thinking a supreme being is nearby guiding me. Don't give up on me, please. I need your strength. I sure like the feeling that you are out there. How do you do it? Help so many, I mean. I have difficulty keeping myself going. Well, I'd better get on with helping myself."

Randy turned his feet toward home, then turned back. "Thanks for listening."

An old man with a cane stepped into his view. Looking around he asked, "Who were you talking to?"

"A pal of mine."

"You meet him here often?"

"Yes, I do."

The old man chuckled. "You might want to check into that, young man."

CHAPTER 23

Squatters Corners
February 2013

Now it would seem logical that big things would happen in the big city during the winter months, and that a place like Squatters Corner would be desolate and abandoned. Not so.

On the blustery night of February 9th, a visitor to a local family had decided to ride a snowmobile through the village. Certainly he thought no one would be out around midnight.

Suddenly, car lights flashed behind the swirling snow. The man on the snowmobile swerved to avoid what seemed like a monster. Turning quickly, the snowmobile flipped over, pinning the driver underneath. There would be no more alcohol or midnight rides for the rider. The weight of the snowmobile had crushed his skull.

The white knuckles that had been gripping the steering wheel of the car had lost control. The automobile hit the edge of the road and ran up a snow bank, flipping over and crushing the rooftop.

Lights were turned on throughout the village. People were running from every house. The noise they heard could only be one thing.

Doc was first on the scene. Thank goodness, he had shoved his cell phone in his jacket pocket. Arriving at the wreck, he dialed the police emergency number. He could see there would be no help for the snowmobile rider, so he concentrated on the occupant of the car. The driver was unconscious, but alive.

Then he heard a whimper from the back seat of the car. Someone flashed a light into the face of a small child clutching a stuffed bear and the corner of a blanket. Carefully, they extracted her from the car. "She must have been asleep on the seat. That's probably what saved her."

"Papa?"

Doc said, "Yes, someone is on the way to help him."

Again he used his phone. "Babs, it's Doc. There's been a terrible accident. I'm sure one of the drivers will go into the hospital. The problem is there is a young child. I'll have the men in the unit check her, but she seems fine. If there seems to be no injury, could you look after her overnight?"

"I'll be right there."

Paramedics from the Emergency Unit were moving the man into their vehicle and had pronounced the child in good shape when lights rounded the corner. Babs's father was driving and Doc could see Billy's face pressed against the back window.

Babs was out of the car before it had fully stopped. She didn't look like a Barbie doll on this encounter. Her hair was a mess. She wore an out-of-shape old winter jacket. Her nightshirt hung over her clumsy boots.

The crowd made a path for her. She reached for the child and folded the bear, blanket, and curly-headed girl inside her jacket. Kissing her on top of her head, Babs held the child against her warm body.

No words were exchanged. She turned and headed toward the car that would take the four of them home.

One of the unit men inquired, "Who was that?"

Doc turned to him. "Haven't you ever seen an angel before?"

Doc began to shiver. Was it because he had neglected to put his boots on? Or was it because he hated the scenario that accompanied disasters? All the lights were repeating their blood-red design on the snow, reflecting in the crowd of faces. These faces were his people. He knew they looked to him for leadership.

Closing his eyes, he silently pleaded, "Please, give me the strength and wisdom that I do not possess at this time."

With that he climbed in beside the driver of the emergency vehicle. At least it was warm inside.

As they pulled away he caught sight of a lone figure heading toward the crowd. He recognized the struggling man. It was the pastor. There was help on the way. He leaned back, relieved he could turn the problem over to someone who could handle it better than he.

CHAPTER 24

Squatters Corners
Early February, 2013

Later that night Doc wandered the halls of the hospital in Livingston. Bright lights, the antiseptic smells detected by his old nose, the whispered talk as he passed the nurses' station; it all brought back forgotten memories. He must stay out of their way in Emergency. It would be easier if he were needed to help. It made him realize how families and friends must feel when waiting.

He was pacing the floor in the waiting room, worrying about a man he knew nothing about. A steady hand touched him on the shoulder. It was his friend the hospital emergency doctor.

"So, our doctor is in from the hills again. According to the ambulance driver, with the heavy snow it's lucky any of you arrived alive. I've been here so many hours I don't know what the weather's like. My replacement couldn't get in. I'm on a double shift. I sometimes wonder if my wife believes me when I call home and explain. Let's sit over here."

As they moved toward a quiet corner Doc remembered how good his own wife had been at understanding the long hours. When he spoke of a patient he was concerned about, she'd listen. It was times like these that he missed her desperately. If only he could go home and she would be there.

"Doc, are you with me?"

"Sorry, I had momentarily stepped backward. How's the man we brought in?"

"Everything has been checked thoroughly. Other than a couple of bruises, we can't find any major injuries. A concussion from the jolt, I'm sure, but no serious damage. However, that may be where the problem lies. We are moving him upstairs to keep close watch for any changes.

"We've put him in a room where the other bed is empty." The doctor stopped to blow his nose. "I do not need this cold.

"There will be nurses checking on him as often as possible, but we're short. If you would keep an experienced eye on him, too, we'd be obliged."

Doc smiled. "Be glad to."

The doctor said the driver's license gave the man's name as Carl Miller from Atlanta, Georgia.

• • •

The continual snow gave the room a faint nightlight. Throughout the night Carl would rest quietly, then fitfully. He would thrash about, calling for someone, before sliding back into sleep again.

Doc moved the sides of the bed up so Carl would not tumble out.

As soon as the shift changed, which brought on fresh and alert minds, he headed to the cafeteria for some breakfast and coffee. Glancing at a wall calendar he realized it was February 10th.

Stopping afterward at the nurses' station, he asked for their thought on Carl's progress. The nurses knew Doc and responded to his questioning without hesitation.

Doc kept shaking his head. "Here we are in the second month of the new year. Where does the time go?"

The nurse smiled, then said, "He keeps calling out a name. It sounds like, 'Manda.' Do you know anything about that Doc?" He'd forgotten about the little girl. Hurriedly he moved down the hall to Carl's room.

He was resting. Doc removed Carl's billfold from his own jacket pocket and began to spread the contents on the bed he had used.

Carl had good medical coverage, thank goodness. Included in a little plastic folder was a picture of him and the little girl. Tucked behind that was a picture of a young woman. She and the child had the same pretty features.

There wasn't much cash and only one major credit card. In with the money was a folded note. It appeared that a friend from Bellingham, Washington, had written to tell Carl that there was work in that area. And he'd be happy to have the two of them stay with him until Carl got on his feet.

"Manda!"

Then Carl's voice became calm. "They promised work. We'll get a place with a yard."

And again he slept.

When the nurse came to check his pulse and temperature Doc walked down the hall to the pay phone. He gave the operator Carl's name and address and asked for the phone number. The phone rang for a long time. He hung up. "God, I wish someone would answer. I need some help here. It's the only lead I have."

Dialing the number again, he refused to hang up. Finally, a woman's voice answered. With great irritation she inquired,

"Who are you trying to reach?"

"Carl Miller."

"He's moved on. I forgot to have this number disconnected."

"Wait! For heaven's sake, don't hang up. Promise me you won't. I'm a doctor. There's been a terrible accident." He told his story.

"Oh no, poor little Manda. Let me sit down a minute and catch my breath. This is awful news."

With that she began to tell what she knew of the man and the little girl. "They rented a small apartment from me. He takes real good care of Manda. His line of work is in building and construction, that kind of stuff. Get's good pay, no bad habits. Guess his wife died a few months after the baby was born. He can't seem to get over it. Packed the little girl up, and with few belongings came this way.

"The building industry was stable for awhile then tapered off. He got restless when there wasn't constant work. Said he'd heard from a man in the Seattle area that things were going steady there. So off they went.

"You say he's unconscious? When he comes to, tell him he and Manda are in my prayers." Before hanging up she gave Doc her phone number and asked to hear about Carl's progress.

Doc replaced the receiver with a more positive feeling. At least there was something to go on.

Returning to the room he drummed up a few prayers of his own, thanking God he was able to be helpful when others needed him. Several times Carl reached out as if searching for something. Doc would hold his hand, and it seemed to calm the man.

The weather cleared considerably as the day progressed. Doc

awoke from dozing in his chair by Carl's bedside to see Babs and Manda standing in the doorway.

Manda rushed forward and took Carl's hand. "Papa, still sleeping?" Doc nodded yes.

He and Babs stepped to the far side of the room. They spoke in hushed tones, watching to see it the girl's presence would cause a reaction in Carl.

"How's it going, Babs?"

"Fine, except now Billy wants a baby sister. He's the one who took her under his wing. No change here?"

"Not so far. It has the doctor concerned."

"Why don't you ride home with us? Get a good night's sleep, a shower, a change of clothes? You can come back in the morning."

"Good idea. I'll notify the staff, so they'll know where to reach me." In the doorway he turned around. "Say, you aren't trying to tell me that I don't seem . . . fresh, are you?" He headed down the hallway smiling. This young woman had given him a lift up. She had rejuvenated his spirit and had gotten his mind out of the hospital waiting mode. He must thank her for her thoughtfulness.

Doc was disappointed when he arrived back at the hospital on Monday to find no change. The doctor came in and talked with Doc about the case, and they discussed new information. That's when they heard a stirring in the bed and saw Carl's eyes open. He appeared to be fairly alert, so the doctor approached him. "Well, Carl Miller, how are you faring this fine morning?"

Carl looked at both men. It was obvious that he was totally confused.

The doctor spoke again. "According to the picture on your driver's license you are Carl Miller." The man scowled and held the puzzled look. Taking a deep breath he struggled to sit up. Both men reached to assist him, propping pillows behind his back.

The look remained. He searched both faces. "Who are you?"

The doctor had had a decent night's sleep and felt more himself, so his humor had been revived. "Not fair, you first."

The man shrugged. "The name doesn't ring a bell, but I do feel like my bell has been rung. Where am I? What happened?"

When the name Manda was mentioned Carl sat upright. He made a fist as if trying to grasp the name and association. Then he ran his hand through his hair as if to make the connection.

Doc handed him the billfold and went through the contents with him. He didn't mention the phone call to Atlanta. You could see Carl's inward struggle to remember and how it upset him that he was failing to put things together.

Then Carl looked alarmed. "If I have a daughter, where is she? Is she alright?"

Doc assured him that she wasn't harmed and that she was being well cared for. Carl leaned back against the pillows, completely worn out.

The doctor immediately ordered a light meal for the patient. "It may not help your memory, but it will bring your body back around." He instructed the nurse to remove the intravenous tubes.

He paused a minute, then spoke to the nurse again. "I want him on his feet this afternoon, more than once."

Putting his fingers to his chin he turned to Doc. "He needs some rebuilding, but he's physically sound. Maybe it would do us all good not to know who we were once in awhile.

"Didn't you tell me you had a spare bedroom in your upstairs?

Would you consider going home to get some rest, and could you take on a temporary boarder? It might do you both good. I hear you're a good man in the kitchen. Carl needs tasty victuals and it will give you someone to look after. I know I'm being pushy here. Would you be willing?"

Doc thought about the situation and nodded yes.

"Come in tomorrow for him. We'll have him in fair shape. I think the accident was one thing too many. It put his body in a state of shock. He needs a few days of complete rest."

The doctor started coughing. "I need to take a couple of days off. Would it be possible to get Carl closer to his daughter? I surmise that seeing her, being under your care, residing in Squatters Corner, and time will cure this fellow and restore his life. It will probably even make it considerably better."

Smiling he said, "You see Carl, Squatters Corner is a cure-all health spa.

"Those are my instructions." As the doctor left the room, Carl, Doc, and the nurse couldn't help but laugh.

The nurse stated, "I haven't seen this side of him for awhile."

Doc caught up with him down on second floor. "I like the way you work, doctor."

In a serious tone the doctor said, "As you know, I made it sound simple. If we're lucky that will be true, but it also could be a lengthy, disappointing process.

"Call me every day with a report. All that was a hopeful guess. We don't want anything to go wrong. That little girl needs her dad.

"By the way, Doc, my wife recently informed me we are expecting." With that, he walked briskly through the swinging doors.

CHAPTER 25

Squatters Corners
Tuesday, February 12, 2013

On the ride to Doc's, Carl had questions. "What was I doing out here in the country?"

"I must apologize, but I went through your billfold hunting for clues. It looks like a friend wrote you about coming to the Seattle area where work seemed more plentiful. I'd guess you were tired, and with the blowing snow you got off the main road. Because of the late hour, maybe you were looking for a place to stay."

Carl sat back in his seat. "It's hard not knowing if what you surmise is fact or fiction."

They made the balance of the trip in silence.

On Saturday night, before they had towed the car away, the men from the towing company had removed anything salvageable. They discovered a couple of large duffle bags. Manda's had a tag on it with her name in bold letters. One of the police officer had dropped that off at Babs's. She found that it contained a few items of clothing. They were plain, but adequate and clean.

The other bag was dropped off at Doc's closed-in back porch. It was the same story: little clothing but enough, mostly work outfits. One encouraging bit was a checkbook and savings account record from the bank in Georgia. Apparently Carl was not without funds but preferred traveling light.

At home Doc assisted the still-weakened Carl, up the stairs. "I hung your clothing in the closet. There's a nice bathroom up here. My wife had insisted on that when we fixed up the place. Wish she could have enjoyed the house longer. I miss her something fierce, but it helps if I keep active. Sure hope you don't sleepwalk. The wife didn't want to hide the wooden steps with carpeting. It's funny what pleases a woman."

Carl rested most of the day. The ordeal had caught up with him. He was up a few times, and Doc prepared chicken and refrigerator biscuits for the evening meal.

After supper when Carl headed up for bed, Doc reminded him, "If you need anything, anything at all, give me a call."

Doc sat staring into space. Maybe the doctor was right: having someone in the house again would be good for him, too. Maybe it would finish an adjustment for himself that he had never completed.

The next day Babs and Manda stopped by. "Papa, Papa. Is this the place? It has a nice yard and trees and even a porch swing."

Carl looked bewildered. Babs said, "I've tried to explain that because of the accident you might not remember things."

"I appreciate what you're doing. I just don't know . . ."

"I understand. Do you believe?"

"I don't know what you mean."

"I'm speaking of religious beliefs."

"You got me there. I may not know the answer to that question even when I figure out the regular stuff."

"That question is a tough one for me, too. I just thought it might provide a guideline for you. Maybe we could work on that one together."

For some reason she wanted this human being to be whole again. Maybe God wanted her to help Manda and her father to regain their lives.

CHAPTER 26

Squatters Corners
Mid-February, 2013

A couple more days of complete rest, good food, and pleasant company was the best medicine for Carl. As he and Doc sat at the supper table Carl said, "I must find work and get things in order here. What do you suppose I did for a living?"

"Looking at your hands makes me think that you spent time outside doing hard physical labor."

"I'm pulling a blank on that one. There are a couple of people I need to repay for services rendered."

"I don't think either of those people is looking for a payback. In fact, I think they would be offended, but some nice gesture for the young woman would be appreciated, I'm sure."

"Any suggestions? I'm not much good in that department."

Just then a knock came at the back door. In tumbled Babs, Billy, and Manda, all covered with snow. Three "Sorrys" echoed through the warm kitchen.

Carl piped up, "Fresh snow, delivered. I don't know if the business will be a go. But the personnel are a jolly bunch."

Everyone present was delighted to hear Carl's response to the situation. Apparently he had a sense of humor.

Manda slipped off her damp coat and handed it to Doc. Carl noted, "She's always adjusted to new people easily."

Doc and Babs looked at one another, but said nothing. Babs introduced Billy.

Manda piped up, "Read story."

Carl said, "Oh, you found your book in your things. That's good. Let's go in on the sofa and I'll read to you."

"No! Me you."

"That's right, you know this one and you like to read it to me, I forgot."

Manda took her dad's hand and started up the stairs. "Bedtime story."

"I do have my pajamas and robe on, but it's a bit early."

"You need rest, Papa."

Carl turned. Everyone was following them on the stairway. "Is it open season on bedtime stories?" Three faces smiled at him with impish looks. Doc blurted out, "A reader like this is a crowd pleaser. No one has read me a bedtime story in a good many years."

As they climbed the rest of the way, Babs and Doc were picking up on Carl's memory pattern. They both smiled. It was possible that the loss would be short term. What a relief that would be.

Mandy insisted Carl climb into bed. She then cuddled up beside him. She knew all the animal sounds as she told about the farmyard. All eyes danced with delight.

"Tuck him in now, Billy." Billy hurried to the other side to help, folding the blankets up around Carl's chin.

Doc sent the troupe on their way with a shiny red apple in each pocket. Then he decided to turn in himself. There was a book he was trying to finish and he liked reading in bed. When he started to turn out the lights he heard the soft voice from above.

"Doc, could I talk to you for a few minutes?"

A solemn silhouette was outlined by a full moon shining in the upstairs window.

"It's starting to happen isn't it? Automatically I'm beginning to remember little things. I was so afraid, but it's coming through. How do I say thank you?"

"By getting well, son, by getting well."

It must have been two o'clock when Doc heard Carl screaming. Doc hit the stairs running. Carl was sitting up when Doc reached his bedside.

"It's okay, Carl." Doc turned on the little bedside lamp. Carl was wet with sweat.

"Was it the accident?"

"Yes, it was like it was happening right now. I hadn't felt it before. At the hospital they told me what happened, but it was like it happened to someone else. Poor Manda. She is alright, isn't she Doc?"

"Oh, yes. The whole town has adopted her."

"How big is this place?"

Doc laughed. "One hundred and two now. What were you doing here at that late hour?"

"It kept getting later. I had driven too long. I was beyond being tired. The snow kept up that mesmerizing effect of shooting at me. Somehow I strayed from the main highway. I had no idea where I was. I knew I needed to stop but it seemed like I had left the world I knew behind. I would have pulled off, but all there was was snow and darkness. Then this dark object with one light crossed my path. That's it."

"Let me get you a dry pair of pajamas. You going to be all right now?"

"Why is everyone being so nice to us?"

Doc smiled. "Just lucky, I guess." After returning with the pajamas Doc told about his conversation with Carl's former landlady.

The following day Doc not only called in his good news to the doctor, but he also phoned Georgia. The landlady appreciated the call and the wonderful news of expected recovery. He told her Carl was thankful for her kind thoughts and prayers.

• • •

On Saturday Doc drove Carl past the school, making an excuse that he needed to speak to one of the workers. "They're putting on a small addition. Mostly volunteer help." He walked to the back of the building.

Carl was out of the car in a second. He walked up to a young man standing at the base of a ladder. "Could I be of some help?"

"I wish someone would. I'm willing to help but I'm scared of heights. This equipment all goes up there. You got any ideas?"

"Sure do. You tell me what goes where. This kind of stuff doesn't bother me. I'm used to it."

The boy was about to thank him when Carl started pumping his hand and thanking him. "In fact, I'm excited about the opportunity."

Doc was speaking to his friend when he heard a familiar voice coming from the rooftop. "Say there, do you want me to start on the roof project? Looks like the supplies are in place. Or aren't you ready for that yet?"

All work stopped. A sea of faces looked upward. Someone called out, "Doc, is that Manda's dad?"

"That's him."

"Well, son-of-a gun. Get down here, lad, and meet the crew. Maybe you can make things gel. We are workin' hard but our organizing stinks. We need a straw boss." With that there were introductions all around and a multitude of smiles.

When they took a break Carl said, "Gentlemen, a word of advice; you're dressed wrong for this kind of work. It wastes too much of your energy trying to keep warm. What do you say to quitting at three o'clock? Then during the week, if the men who could best explain what you want to accomplish could meet with me, well, we could be ready to steamroll this job by next Saturday."

One of the men spoke up. "You can tell us the rest next week, but tell us what to wear today so we can be rarin' to go when we gather next weekend."

Doc's original plan had been to take Carl for a ride to show him the community. That would not be necessary. How could just driving one's car back in the garage make a man feel so good? Things were beginning to change in Squatters Corner. Doc couldn't resist sending a letter to Randy explaining the current happenings.

On Sunday Doc, Carl, Manda, Babs, Billy, and Gramps took up a whole pew at church. You never saw so many smiles, so much hand-shaking. Anyone glancing down would say, "That's not the Squatters Corner I know. What's the big celebration?"

As the six of them left the church Billy said, "They're coming for dinner, aren't they, Gramps?"

He patted Billy on the top of the head. "By gosh, it's a good thing you said that. I'm getting forgetful of my manners in my old age.

"Your mom's got a large roast beef with potatoes, carrots, and onions in the oven. Plenty for two more hungry people. Join us, gentlemen.

"If I remember right, Babs has whipped up something special for dessert. I believe she called it raspberry surprise."

Babs blushed with the old man's praise. He continued to speak. "You need to spend more time with your daughter, Carl."

"I've got to find us a place to stay. Is there anything you know of close by?"

Both Babs and Doc tried to cover up a gasp at Carl's statement. He and Manda would be staying at The Corners, at least for a while?

At the farmhouse Manda followed her papa like a stray puppy. If he sat down, she was on his lap. You could tell that Billy was sorry he had asked about inviting the two. Manda usually trailed around behind him. They had become constant companions. He was her protector. Now he had been reduced back to being a little boy. Why didn't the men leave?

CHAPTER 27

**Coeur d'Alene and Squatters Corners
March, 2013**

By March the public's response to Randy's book was not overwhelming, but the result was satisfactory. His publishers encouraged him to start a second one. His new book would be about Montana and a small village in the mountains. He felt compelled to do it. The hard part would be to keep it fictitious.

By the second week Randy was restless and couldn't hide it. As the four of them sat at the table one evening Jill popped the question.

"The book is about Montana, isn't it?"

Randy almost hung his head.

"That's the story that's in my heart. I think the only way to move on is to write it."

"When are you leaving?"

Randy jerked his head up. "I'm doing it here."

"You won't do it justice if you try to write it here."

"It's not right to go this time, Jill."

All three were smiling. "We can manage, Dad."

Trish spoke up. "This one had better be super good because the three of us know what you're writing about. We'll be tough critics."

Jill was still smiling but her eyes were glistening.

Jill and Randy were so proud of the kids and the way they were developing into fine young people. Trish's and Danny's ability to adjust to different circumstances was a plus for the future, but the separation would hurt, and they all knew it.

Last time was wise; was it this time? His work would be predominant this trip . . . but still.

• • •

When Randy stepped off the bus in Squatters Corner this time, the weather was balmy and felt good.

But something was wrong. When pulling up he experienced an eerie feeling in his bones. Then he realized part of the problem. The whole town was dark. Maybe it was an electrical outage. But there was absolutely no movement. And the feeling remained. The strange stillness was there, like an overcast of doom.

Then a figure moved away from the bus station and came to help move Randy's things. It was Doc. He said nothing. It was as if he was unable to speak.

Randy's legs and arms felt like Jell-O.

"Let's go over here and sit on the bench for a few minutes," said Doc.

Thoughts of one disaster after another were taking shape in Randy's mind. He was afraid to voice the question.

Doc began by saying, "I'll load your stuff and take you home later." There was no sense stalling. "More than one sadness has come to our mountain.

"Merry was killed last evening. It appears that it was a tragic accident followed by Joey's destroying himself."

Randy peered through the darkness at the person next to him. This had to be a bad dream.

Doc leaned forward as if even the telling was too much.

"That's not all." After an extended pause he added, "Shawn was killed in a horse accident in late January."

Randy lurched to his feet and staggered to the side of the building. He was retching violently, but Doc let him be. Too big a dose of horrendous news and no antidote. After a few minutes Randy staggered back and sat down on the bench. The bile taste in his mouth felt like it came from the pits of hell.

"Doc, why didn't you contact us in January? My family will be shattered."

"I didn't know at the time if you'd ever return to us. I cannot remember how many times I called your number and hung up, or how many times I began a letter to you and then pulled back. I try to do things right, but sometimes I fail miserably. I am so terribly sorry."

"I know how you must feel. Sometimes life is unbearable. You'd like to think things would always be good and it just doesn't work out.

"I need to call Jill. She'll want to be here. Poor little Merry."

"She's on her way. We called your house. That's how we knew you were coming. She's called her folks to stay with Trish and Danny. She was terribly upset."

After they arrived at the cabin Doc spoke more of Shawn.

"That turned out to be a haunting situation."

"Haunting?"

"Her parents stepped forward, and she was buried in a matter of hours. The community was informed by their lawyer that there was to be no service of any kind. No observance was to be held. It was over, finished."

"Where do these precious parents of hers reside?"

"They're the Winslows. No one has seen either of them since that day. The house is locked and abandoned. There is not even a caretaker on the property. It's weird and scary. All kinds of strange stories have been circulated. There is a mist that hangs over the house. Odd lights in the night. Ghostly noises. No doubt there are looters, although I don't know how they get in. They say there are heavy chains and padlocks on all the doors. It's like a bad mystery story. Most people stay clear of the place. Most did anyway."

Standing and pacing the floor in disbelief Randy muttered, "No wonder she had problems and was afraid of life.

"Trish will be so sad. She had received a nice note from Shawn thanking her for the Christmas remembrance. She had said she was looking . . . forward . . . to . . . What really happened?"

"Tell you what, we need to set that aside for now. Our priority must be Merry."

With that Randy sat back down. "So, let's get on with the problem at hand." Knowing he had to do that calmed him down some.

Doc filled in Randy with as many facts as he could. Other than that it was a lot of surmising from the police, Doc, and the community.

CHAPTER 28

Squatters Corners
Saturday, March 9, 2013

It had not been time for the store to close, but Mr. and Mrs. Krismus had suggested Merry head home and they'd close up. Their house was in the next block over.

Merry walked slowly, enjoying the break in the weather. It indicated another good spring for her. Her life had turned out differently than she had expected. She was extremely thankful.

She heard the truck coming. Joey pulled over by the curb. "Could I give you a lift, Merry?" It was not his usual tone, but soft and melancholy.

"Now, Joey, I just live around the corner."

"Aw, come on, Mer, give a guy a break."

She sighed, and against her better judgment started toward the truck. Joey got out slowly, walked around and held the door open for her, a perfect gentleman. She was impressed as he assisted her up into the cab.

Merry thought she smelled a trace of liquor on his breath. She hoped she was mistaken.

Joey walked around and got back in the driver's seat. He looked at her with a soft smile. Then, whooping and hollering, he shifted gears and drove out of town.

"Please, Joey, take me home," she stated calmly.

"No, sir, I've wanted to outsmart and capture you for a long time, my Merry."

He didn't sound mean or threatening, but desperate for companionship and someone to understand. Merry wondered if he had picked her because they were both misfits.

He pulled into his yard. Then Joey jumped out the driver's door and ran over to Merry's side and threw open the door. He picked her up and carried her into the sitting room and deposited her on the couch.

"You're light as a feather, Merry."

"Joey, I need to go home. Mr. and Mrs. Krismus will be worried about me."

"Naw, you're a grown up girl, pretty little Merry."

Merry sat quietly, not really having a clue as to how to get out of such a predicament. She was usually a clever person, but she had never imagined a situation like this.

"Something to drink, Merry?"

"No thank you. I really do need to get on home. Please, Joey."

"I never have company, Merry. Would you like some cheese and crackers, or Oreo cookies? I don't know how to entertain. How about if I light a candle? I like candles. Good thing, they are going to shut off my electric. I'll put some music on. You'll like that, I know. I'll turn it down just for you. I usually play it loud. I even have some pretty stuff that belonged to Unc."

Merry remained stiffly seated. She couldn't even come up with any conversation. She was afraid to move for fear of his reaction. She knew now that he had been drinking for quite a while. There were half-empty bottles strewn all over the room.

Joey stood in the doorway with a newly opened bottle of beer. "They say you can't mix drinks but it don't bother me. Sure you don't want somethin'?" He began to slur his words and cackle at whatever he said.

"You're usually a fun person, Merry. What's the matter with you?" He moved into the room. All of a sudden he threw the bottle toward one of the sitting room windows. The window shattered as the bottle shot through it and smashed on the porch.

This brought Merry to action. Jumping from the couch she headed toward the kitchen. "I'll get a broom and clean that up for you."

Joey grabbed her from behind and lifted her into his arms again. "I didn't bring you here to sweep up."

Moving into the bedroom he laid her on the bed and leaned over her.

"Please, Joey, take me home." There were tears in her eyes.

"There's some things I'd like to try."

"No . . . Joey . . . please."

He was undoing his belt buckle as she pleaded. Pulling it loose from his last belt loop he whipped it at her, slapping her face hard. That would scare her and she'd want to please him. This wasn't as much fun as he thought it would be.

Looking at her again he saw blood on her forehead. "Merry, you okay?" She lay completely still. "Merry?' He could see he'd got her with the big heavy buckle, the one he'd won at the carnival, the one he was so proud of. "Merry, talk to me, I'm sorry." He touched her arm, and he knew he'd killed her.

Sitting down in a chair Joey bowed his head. Slowly he got up. He gathered all the candles in the house and he climbed the stairs.

He hesitated in front of a door. Finally he reached for the knob.

It had been his aunt's room. It was the only nice room in the house. All other rooms had died of neglect years ago. It was a pretty room. Setting up all the candles was the first thing.

Then he ceremoniously carried Merry up and laid her upon the quilted bedspread. He wiped the blood from her head and straightened her dress. He walked to his aunt's dresser and picked up her soft brush and fluffed Merry's hair on the sides. Returning the brush to its place he glanced at the mirrored reflection on the scene he had created. Turning, with great sadness he completed his task.

Carefully he removed the lace curtains from the window and covered Merry's body. This was a shrine.

After lighting all the candles he seated himself in a chair beside the bed. Beautiful Merry. No doubt his only friend. In his own way, he had loved her. Joey could not forget the tears glistening in her eyes as she had asked him to take her home. If he had, this day would have ended differently.

Joey knew there was only one possible ending to this day. He walked downstairs and out to the barn, then he returned to Merry's bedside. He needed to say good-bye. He returned to the barn with his uncle's old gun and shot himself.

• • •

Mr. and Mrs. Krismus had taken immediate action when they arrived home and discovered that Merry was not there. The police at Livingston were called. When people began to hear of Merry's disappearance, someone claimed that they had seen Joey's truck speeding out of town.

"We'd better not condemn someone without proof," a local man advised.

As the police drove past Joey's, they spied his truck, with both doors open, parked by the house. A townsman riding with them informed them that without fail Joey always put the truck away in the garage. He'd claimed it was the only thing Joey took care of.

The officer turned the police car around and drove up behind the truck. Reaching to knock on the back door they discovered it wasn't latched. Pushing it open slowly, they called out but there was no reply.

The sitting room was dark except for the light from the tape deck. There were bottles and cans lying everywhere. One of the policemen motioned toward the stairs where he could see flickering lights.

As they stepped into the scene in the bedroom there was an eerie silence. It was like a scene from a horror movie. Each man removed his hat; nothing was said. Eventually the police were able to pull themselves out of the room. Returning to the car, they called forensics detectives to come out and document the crime. The police waited in the yard next to the squad car, each contemplating sleepless nights and nightmares. Each yearning for a world where people lived happily ever after.

CHAPTER 29

Squatters Corners
Sunday, March 10, 2013

Merry's funeral was to be in two days. The lights returned to the town, but the spirit had not. People were conducting their business in hushed tones. Jill, Sally, and Roy had arrived.

Not a word was spoken as people filed into the church. The piano was even toned down.

It looked like the pastor was going to rise and take his place behind the pulpit. However, at that very moment the front door opened and a little gentleman walked down the center aisle. Billy scooted in and looked up at Randy, who motioned that his lap was available. As he settled in, the boy reached over and took hold of Jill's hand for a moment. She had all she could do not to flee from the church in tears. This whole situation was charged with emotions.

Again, it appeared that the pastor was preparing to lumber to his place. But a clear young voice piped up. Billy was not speaking loudly, but even the slightest whisper could have been heard.

"My mom said I could come even though I'm missing school. She knows how much Merry and I liked each other. Merry liked everybody, but I think she and I were very good friends. Maybe because we were both little. She was even called a Little Person, did you know that?

"Mom pressed my white Sunday shirt and made sure my good pants were clean. She said I had to wear my bow tie and she slicked my hair down with water so Merry would notice how nice I looked.

"I wore my cowboy boots 'cause they were Merry's favorite. She said if I got too big for them I could give them to her. Do you think I should give them to her now?"

Randy shook his head no and put his index finger to his lips. He held the boy tightly and clenched his jaw to hold his own composure.

This time the pastor was able to stand. He was the only one who knew that there wasn't a dry eye in the sanctuary.

"Ladies and gentlemen, we are here to help Mr. and Mrs. Krismus get through a tragedy. I do not have to praise Merry, for each of you has been doing that for several years. Her arrival in this town was a blessing. We thank you, Lord, for the time we were able to learn from her. I have before me a paper that lists many of her attributes, but I will not have to use it.

"For someone beat me to it. Her best friend has just given a beautiful tribute that I could not possibly surpass.

"As you rise to join us here at our little cemetery I urge you to remain quiet. It is a nice day, so I opened one of the back windows to let in some fresh air. A white dove landed on the window sill. I think it has come to escort our girl on her journey home."

Billy had fallen asleep. Randy carried him in one arm and held Jill's hand with the other. As Billy woke he asked, "Is she gone now?"

"She's up with the angels. You asked about the boots earlier. Merry would have wanted you to keep them."

"I'll bet Merry will be the cutest angel of all."

Randy lowered him to the ground. "You're heavy, boy. Get on home and tell your mom you were very good."

There would be sandwiches and coffee at Harris's following the service. Merry had been known for miles around. It was Harris's way of honoring a special member of the community.

Randy turned to Jill. "A year ago I would have asked to walk home by myself, through the woods. But under the circumstances I think we should go together. I'd like to skip the get-together afterward. Is that okay with you?" In answer, she put her arm around his waist and they started off.

● ● ●

After most of mourners had left the cemetery, the pastor and several of the men from farthest away remained. The cemetery was small, but there were large shrubs throughout, thus no one noticed the second gravesite that had been prepared early that morning. The pastor accompanied the men as they carried the plain casket. There were no flowers. Nor had there been any requests to spend a minute alone with the deceased. Joey was buried beside his uncle.

The pastor could think of little to say. But he did ask if the Lord would grant Joey a more peaceful existence than he had spent here on earth.

CHAPTER 30

Squatters Corners
Wednesday, March 13, 2013

The afternoon following the funeral Jill looked out the window and called Randy to her side. "I take it that's Miss Lydia."

He took her hand and said, "Come, you must meet her. I think of her as a dream-weaver."

As they approached Lydia laid her paint brush aside. "I was hoping you would spot me."

Randy said, "You know why I'm here."

Before answering she made other comments. "Usually I don't make it out this early. This weather is rare. But I bundled, and I'll get a different concept of the scenery. I usually think of it in midsummer only. Which is not a good thing for a painter to admit. Shame on me.

"I have brought a couple of extra folding seats and light blankets if you need them for your shoulders. The grass has dried, but the ground is too damp to sit on. I need to speak to both of you."

Jill found the woman intriguing.

"Before I tell you what happened the day we lost Shawn, I want to get something straight. Through my lifetime I have often suffered from gossip. Some of it was true, most not. Some hurt. Once in a while it was downright amusing. Often times it was created by my own imagination. I was sure people were talking about me when, in fact, they probably didn't know I existed, or couldn't care less. We are our own tormentors."

She sat watching the clouds and then continued, looking straight into Jill's eyes. "Your husband is a very likeable and handsome man. Shawn loved him: she told me of her feeling toward him."

Randy scowled and stiffened. Holding her hand up, Lydia said, "Let me finish."

Miss Lydia was still holding Jill's full attention, not because of the statement but because of her presentation.

"I'm not speaking of sexual love or an affair. I'm talking about deep friendship.

"She was a lovely young woman. I imagine the attraction would have been there in the beginning under any circumstance. The fact that Randy was here trying to get himself back together made the feeling stronger. Shawn had been working on that for so long herself.

"She was not looking for a happiness to return to but to establish a center that she could work out from. Embedded in her was the ugly fact that not one person had cared about her. From the day she was conceived there was no feeling of love for her."

Miss Lydia intensely studied the clouds again. Picking up her brush, she worked on the painting again, touching up details. Then, appearing to speak to herself, she spoke again. "The painting Shawn did for you folks . . . She insisted I help her with the clouds in the background. Clouds were her downfall. She wanted it to seem to be alive."

Bowing her head she admitted, "If Shawn had been mine she

would never have spent one day without love. Her life would have been so different. Mine too. Some people slip away, and you are saddened. But you go on about your business. Yet when you are associated with the person oftentimes you question God's reasoning.

"But we can't run things; that job belongs to a higher power. I imagine all our lives would be different if we were the planner. We're probably better off this way. The man upstairs can see farther than we can. Still, I do think we have a lot to do with our own destiny."

With this she looked at Randy. "Think of the change in your life because of your stop-off here. I must warn you," she smiled. "This will not be your last visit."

Randy studied the deep penetration of her eyes.

Miss Lydia continued. First she spoke directly at Jill to make clear that there had been a feeling between Shawn and Randy. Then she made sure that Jill understood about their relationship, explaining that Shawn would have done nothing to harm her or Trish and Danny. She thought they were a wonderful family.

According to Miss Lydia, part of Shawn's attraction was that Randy treated her as a friend. There were men who had approached her with only one thing in mind. Even at the stables there were husbands who propositioned her. She felt that a man was something to avoid, to be leery of. Randy was a person she could talk to. How nice to find someone she could trust. He was the first man she had felt comfortable with. It had given her peace for the first time in her life.

"What had happened that day in January? Most of it is a guess. There was a witness but he only confused matters.

"Old Will was hysterical when he came running to a nearby farmhouse. He claimed it was his fault. Said he was under the little bridge when he heard the horse's hooves on the road. When the horse stepped on the bridge, Will jumped out because he was frightened. The horse shied, then reared up.

"Both horse and rider fell into the creek. Shawn lay at the edge of the water. The horse rose to his feet and hobbled over to her. Shawn was dead, whether from hitting her head on the rocks or drowning, we'll never know. The word spread like wildfire. The Winslows arrived at Doc's minutes after the body was brought in."

Refusing an autopsy, they had her buried immediately. Each left, complaining about her getting mixed up with stupid horses. Complaining about her carelessness, and about her not wanting to represent her proper station in life. Doc said their attitude seemed to be that she had wasted a lot of their time and energy.

"A legal paper was delivered to Doc a short time later. It was so full of thee's and thou's that it would have been laughable had it not been about someone everyone cared so much about. No memorial service, no observance. That was one of the reasons no one contacted you. It was treated as if Shawn had never existed. Like we must erase her from our memories. No one is positive where she is buried. It leaves an empty cloud for each of us to deal with. Lots of odd questions and no satisfying answers."

There was a lengthy pause as Miss Lydia doubled up her fists until her knuckles turned white. She closed her eyes and her face turned pale. Then she went on with her story. Randy could tell that she wanted to get the telling of this tale over with.

"Was the episode legal? We are a long way from things out here. If one would protest, it would take forever to get it settled. What good would it do? The outcome would remain the same.

"Yes, us old-timers knew who she was. But if the Winslows wanted to handle it that way it was okay with us. We could keep her secret."

Jill asked, "Why didn't she leave the area?"

"I think she felt too lost and abandoned to strike out. She was timid deep down. She'd never really had a childhood. The few of us who cared tried to encircle her as a family might. Come to think of it, not being able to openly grieve by going through the funeral process probably made it harder for all. No closure. It left an open wound.

"I'm sorry this is taking so long. For my own sake I need to get feelings out in the open.

"They had to shoot the horse. That would have upset Shawn more than her own death. She would have been angry with herself for letting the horse set foot on that slippery surface. It was a nasty day. I'm surprised she was out. She was a cautious rider. There are unanswered questions, as I said. My only hope is now that she is in God's house she knows what love is."

Jill watched as the woman tried to gain her composure.

"By the way, the necklace your daughter gave Shawn—she wore it every day. It was the only piece of jewelry I ever saw her take to." Miss Lydia halted her story.

"My friend at the stable discovered it lying on the dresser the following day."

The three of them remained silent for a few minutes, each wrestling with their own thoughts.

• • •

Lydia then relayed another strange part of the story. The disaster had put Old Will in a nursing home. He was clean and well fed for a change. No one knew if he appreciated that or not. He muttered all the time, but no one could understand him. He never slept. He seemed very distressed about something. The staff wanted to help but did not know how to respond. The one thing they could make out was his constant calling out for Billy.

The manager called Billy's mom and she brought him down to see if he could help his old friend. According to one of the attendants, the relief on Old Will's face was remarkable.

Billy rushed up to the old man and gave him a hug. Will whispered in Billy's ear. Billy put his arm around the old man's shoulder and squeezed. Then he nodded and hurried away.

That night Old Will died.

They had an open-casket visitation at the church. As she told this portion of the story, Lydia chuckled. It seemed that, cleaned and shaven, no one was sure it was Will.

The pastor told those who gathered that he was working in the back of the church the afternoon before they buried Will. Billy came in and went to the front. He got to his knees beside the casket.

The pastor didn't understand Billy's message but he often repeated the story to anyone who would listen. He claimed that Billy said, "I found her, Will. Mrs. Gray is at my house. Mom gave her a warm bath and took a soft towel and made her dry. Then she gave her a saucer of milk. When I left she was asleep on my bed. I'll look after her, don't you worry."

Miss Lydia continued, "I guess when Billy passed the good man he turned and explained. "Had to talk loud, Old Will was near-deaf you know.

"It was said that I used to let Old Will sleep at my place. That was true. When the winter storms would lower the temperature to a single digit I'd let him sleep in the spare room and fill him full of good hot food.

"In his younger days, he used to be a fisherman on the east coast. He never told how come he ended up here. We never questioned each other. Because of our style of life we probably knew more than anyone about the goin's on in the territory. We quietly observed and repeated nothing. I used to bring homeless friends to my apartment in New York also. I'm sure people thought I was free and easy. The deal was I just made darn good soup."

Jill asked Lydia if she would join them for supper.

"Next time you come I'd like that," said Lydia. Then she totally surprised them as she began to weep.

Neither Jill nor Randy was sure how to respond. Miss Lydia lifted her head up. "I want you to do something for me, Randy. You are a writer, and a good one. I read your latest offering, and was impressed.

"Just write an article and make people understand. We know so little about one another. Who were these four people? Were voices whispering or shouting to us for help, for attention? They are gone now. Did we ignore their pleas? Were we too busy to listen for their outcries?

"I listen for the rustle of the trees. But am I shutting out the things I should be aware of, those soft voices that say 'I'm lonely, I'm afraid'? Maybe if people had bothered to take a minute now and then more of us would have known them. Maybe their lives could have been better. Maybe they would still be here. I had special feelings for the two girls, but even I didn't make a supreme effort. Would it have been different if we tried harder? Should we leave people outside the circle? Can we find some way to embrace them even when they seem to want to be left alone?"

Randy stopped her for a minute. "You did help. Probably more than you realized. No matter how we try we can't solve other people's problems. Some of the effort has to come from within. Even with God's guidance problems don't wash away easily.

"You're right, it does deserve an article. A tribute to them. They each left behind lessons for us to learn. It will take research so I can't do it overnight. But one thing I insist on, Miss Lydia: lift the burden from your shoulders. If those are some of the problems, then we all need to share the load."

Randy and Jill helped Lydia pack up her cart, and she allowed the gesture, appearing very tired.

CHAPTER 31

Squatters Corners
Mid-March, 2013

On March 14th Jill left for home.

Randy's research on the four people gone from the community led him to Doc's. But Doc was on his way to the city to visit a favorite patient who was not doing well. "The doctors won't release him from the hospital yet. Too many complications."

They made arrangements for the following day, which would include lunch. Doc also commented that he would catch Randy up on many untold stories and clue him in on some new happenings.

Randy decided that since he was out and about he'd not return to his writing until the 18th. A couple of days off would do him good. As he passed the school he cut into the woods. The smell of spring felt good as it traveled into his system. With it came the reminder of Jill and the kids. His longing for their companionship overpowered him. He turned his feet toward the cabin.

He closed the cabin door and leaned his back against it. He hadn't set a goal for himself. His mind cleared. Tomorrow I'll walk, then spend the afternoon with Doc. I'll hit the novel hard, come Monday. Then he went blank. His thoughts were trailing off to nowhere. *Stop. Stop. Stop. Get reorganized and follow through.* Was this confusion formed because of the deaths? He was rambling, had to get things straightened around. *My reward will be to go home.* The separation between Jill and Randy must not happen again. His motivation was dwindling.

After hot tea and a half a sandwich, Randy went upstairs. Falling on the bed with his clothes on, he slept the night.

• • •

The following morning he headed for the trees. By eleven o'clock he was home. After showering, he took off for Doc's with a lighter step.

Another beginning. He could feel his blood pulsating through his veins. Writing was not a good enough excuse for being separated from his loved ones. He wasn't ashamed, but he knew it was time for some changes.

He arrived at Doc's with glowing cheeks and a purpose. He would wrap up this portion of his life and make decisions on the future.

Doc didn't have to ask any questions. He could see the change. Before him stood a man with conviction.

Just as a greeting he asked, "How's it going, Randy?"

"I'm doing well, Doc. I keep wanting to give you credit, but you say no, it's my own doing. But you must admit you headed me in the right direction. Maybe I should thank the Jeep. I swear it made its own way to your place."

"I like to see you smile. It makes me feel like smiling, too. It doesn't always work that way. I like success stories."

The two of them did the dishes. Doc insisted that Randy dry them and leave them on the counter. He claimed that he was like a fussy housewife; if someone else put things away he couldn't find them for months.

They retreated to comfortable chairs in the small living room. Doc asked if Jill had returned home safely. Then he sighed and said, "I'd like to comment on something that has bugged me about Joey, first off. I was thumbing through a medical journal the other day and came across the word psychopath. The article used some familiar descriptions. It spoke of mental disorder. Joey made it evident that he had no moral principles or restraints. He was antisocial. Seemed to have a lack of ability to love or establish meaningful personal relationships. He regarded himself as the center of all things. Had no regard for the interests, beliefs or attitudes, or feelings of others. And he failed to learn from experience. Sound familiar? The only problem is, we all have some of these habits from time to time. Guess that's my comment on that."

Doc offered tea but Randy shook his head no.

"Now in order to talk about Shawn I need to go back to the very beginning. Most of my information is hand-me-down."

Randy was waiting to hear it all.

"There was no love between Shawn's mother and the lord of the manor. It was understood the marriage was to be a business arrangement. Two wealthy, influential families. Nose-in-the-air stuff. Heavy money. Social prominence. That's why the mansion was constructed. Also the condos nearby. She was positive that their equals would want to have a place of their own, to stay when they came calling.

"You must have noticed the condos have never been lived in. Her ego outweighed her sense. If she summoned, those supposed friends attended, then escaped.

"The parties were worth the time just to experience the splendor. Even my wife and I were invited when we first arrived. We felt it was an afterthought. Guess she took one look at us and decided we weren't going to add to the entertainment factor. However she did spare a fleeting moment to gush over the fact of Squatters Corner having its own doctor. She never called the office, thank goodness. I'm sure we wouldn't have been classy enough to have handled any of their personal problems.

"Their names meant something in Helena, where they resided in their fancy home near the capital building. Out here they impressed no one. She might have thought that the city people would be overwhelmed about socializing in such a unique atmosphere and want to remain a while.

"Rumors leaked from the home staff to the surrounding world. She found it was revolting that her husband should require more from her than arranging dinner parties. She hated him. He would stalk her when his appetite wasn't satisfied in the city. It was usually after partying and he was inebriated. The help said afterward she would cry, and then scream with anger."

Doc wiped his brow with a handkerchief. He rose and headed for the kitchen. He'd fix tea whether they consumed it or not. He hated recalling the different stories. They sounded like something out of a soiled diary you'd find hidden in the remains of a centuries old castle garden. He was sure one could hear the frightened servants scurrying to hide like rats in infested buildings.

Returning with two cups of steaming tea, he found that Randy wasn't faring any better than he was with this information.

Randy sat staring into space. You could see that he, too, had traveled back like it was an ancient movie plot.

"Then doom hit the mansion. The lady was pregnant. She

found the process disgusting. Such a thing was below her station.

"There were no visitors. The whole affair was to be kept secret. The master stayed in the city. It was spread around the social circle that the lady was traveling abroad. Some locals wondered why she didn't have an abortion. According to the girls who were hired to look after her, the mention of the word put her in unbelievable distress. As much as she hated what was happening to her body, and what it would produce, the thought of abortion frightened her. It appeared as though even she had her limits. They said she would cry for hours.

"A doctor came from the city to attend to the big event. The servants claimed that the mother refused to cry out even when the pain was intolerable. The pretty baby girl never cried like a newborn. The girls said it was as if the baby knew that her existence was to be a quiet one.

"The baby was rushed to the far end of the mansion where one of the young girls would look after her. Even the help very seldom caught a glimpse of her. Her birth seemed like something out of the distant past. It was said that as soon as she could walk, a nanny was hired. Neither of the parents would even watch the toddler through the window as she played in the yard. The girl must have become nonexistent. Maybe if it had been a boy, the father would have acted in a different manner. No one knows."

Doc sat back. Sighing, he said, "Do you suppose the story is true?"

Randy moved back in his chair also. He hadn't realized he had been sitting on the edge of his seat. They both appeared to have gone through an ordeal. Slowly he answered.

"It sounds . . . They say truth is stranger than fiction. It is a tale I wish I hadn't heard. She's already passed through life and yet it makes me yearn to enfold her in my arms as an infant and care for her."

"That's only the beginning."

Randy put his hands on each side of his head, almost as if to blot out the telling, but Doc continued.

"The child was almost hidden behind closed doors, like families used to when denying a youngster with physical or mental disability years ago. As soon as possible Shawn was carted off to England and a private school. She was to be provided with good schooling, in addition with good training on how to walk, talk, and dress. How to present herself properly."

Doc went on to tell that years passed and the parents received a letter from the school. It stated that the school had filled its responsibilities and would be returning the young lady to her home. They hoped that Mr. and Mrs. Winslow would be pleased with the results.

"The lady was seething. The husband asked the help to prepare a room for their guest.

"Shawn was a beauty. It appeared to the staff that this young woman, though seeming lost and alone, did know that these were her parents. The mother refused to greet her and retired to her own room. The father acknowledged her presence and turned her over to the help, who showed her upstairs. They brought her dinner meal to the room. She appeared defeated and confused. The father remained in his study, downing glass after glass of substance from his liquor cabinet.

"As the story goes, Shawn prepared for bed. Her door opened and her father stumbled toward her. Luckily he was in bad enough shape that she was able to push him back through the doorway.

Supposedly, the cursing and unsteady movement stopped. After peering into the hallway she tore down the stairs and was out the door into the darkness."

"The servants, helpers, staff—these people so full of stories, why didn't they help her?"

"There are not a lot of places to work out here. They needed their jobs. The pay scale was high, and they were frightened out of their wits. They did their work, accepted their checks, and went home. How many intelligent people do the same every day in their jobs?

"Nonetheless the staff changed frequently, for everyone's safety I imagine. Cruelty at its best. There are many strange situations surrounding us. We like to overlook them. It's easier. Look the other way, and be thankful that our lives are good. Humans are supposed to be the smartest of the world's creatures. I wonder?"

The two men stepped outside to get some fresh air. After a few minutes Doc motioned for them to go back inside.

"Horrible as it sounds, I think I do believe it," Doc said. "There were undoubtedly some embellishments, or some things eliminated; but I have a terrible suspicion that basically that's what happened.

"I need to complete this, then I have a happy story to relate."

"I'm glad you have saved the happy one 'til last. I have a feeling this one is going to grab onto me for too long a time. So, Shawn ran from a molesting father and a mother who was cruel and had zero compassion."

"I am surmising some of the balance of the story. But most of it is the truth told to me by people who I know well.

"It was raining hard. Shawn apparently had no idea as to where she was. When the thunder and lightning began she must have spotted the barn way ahead. Ginger Beal, the stable owner, saw her go into the barn through the side door. She'd been up to the bathroom and was watching the storm from her bedroom window. Ginger told me her part of the story one day when she was asking me about a medication.

"Ginger claimed that Shawn was sitting on a bale of hay, crying her eyes out, and looking like a drowned mouse. When she calmed down she told Ginger that her last employer had tried to molest her and she had run.

"Ginger pretty much guessed who the girl was, although she gave her name as Shawn Winston. Ginger asked whether she knew anything about horses. With that the girl's face lit up. Then she asked Shawn if she would like to come to the house for a warm shower and hop in a spare bed for the night.

"The following morning things were settled. Shawn boasted that she had worked with horses for several years and was an efficient trainer. Ginger put her to work that morning. Then she sent a young stable hand to collect Shawn's belongings.

"Shawn always appeared . . . correct. Ms. Beal was short and stocky. She had graying hair. Usually she wore baggy pants, one of her husband's old shirts, and tall rubber boots. But no one noticed because the glow from her heart shone so bright.

"She quickly arranged for a snug apartment to be constructed on the second floor of the horse barn. It became Shawn's home. Ginger's husband had died several years back, so she appreciated Shawn's help.

"Ginger and Miss Lydia had been friends for years. So that's where she came into the picture. Shawn's life was much improved toward the end."

Randy shook his head. "Unbelievable. Guess you and I don't know what lonely is."

Doc rose to his feet. "Let's take three deep breaths to clear those frightening tales from our memories."

• • •

Then Doc began sharing information with Randy about the surprise boarder who had arrived during a winter storm and his little girl Manda.

CHAPTER 32

Squatters Corners
April–May, 2013

R andy had worked long, hard hours on the article Miss Lydia requested about Merry, Joey, Shawn, and Old Will. Combining her thoughts and his philosophical ideas, it covered the touching questions of, Do we know ourselves, let alone others? How many wonderful individuals do we miss? What a shameful waste.

He'd sent it to the *Mountain Review* at the beginning of April. They published it the following week. It was so beautifully written that it was picked up by bigger papers across the country.

The money he received was good, but he couldn't accept it for his own use. He'd made a quick trip to Miss Lydia's, and they had decided to deposit it in a separate fund in the bank. They would set it aside for a special unknown project in the foreseeable future to benefit the community.

Randy had been so busy on his novel that the passing of weeks had slipped by him. The story in his mind had enveloped him. He had become someone else. Becoming a player in his own novel was not healthy, and he knew it.

Realizing he had to get back to the real world, he pressed Save, then shut his computer down. He turned on the radio in the kitchen and was shaken when he heard the date. Where had the time gone?

Running out the door, he headed for Doc's. Randy was so out of breath when he arrived that the nurse rushed him into one of the examining rooms. Doc came bustling in seconds later.

"What is it, Randy?"

"I've let too much time elapse. I haven't been communicating with people."

"We just spent an afternoon together on Saturday."

"What's today?"

"Thursday, the 25th. My office day."

"Why am I mixed up?"

"I'm going to send the nurse in to check your vital signs. I'll finish up with my other patient and be back in a few minutes. Just relax."

When Doc returned he was smiling. "Looks like you'll pull through. Now what seems to be the difficulty? Let's start with this question: How's the book coming?"

"I've been pushing, trying to move the story along, so I can go home."

"Do you have a deadline to meet?"

"No, but I need to be with my family."

Doc leaned back in his chair, studying Randy carefully.

"So, what's keeping you here? Did you say you wanted to complete it before you left? If you've been doing it by the speed method I'll bet it's a boring read."

"How did you know?"

"The whole town has been concerned about the lights in the cabin at late hours. They figure you have abandoned them."

Randy folded his arms across his chest.

"What's the matter with me?"

"I'd diagnose it as homesickness."

They both laughed and Randy breathed a sigh of relief.

"So, I lost my place in time. Why?"

"It happens to all of us. Our priorities get out of order. Why don't you go home for a visit, then come back and finish up?"

"No, I'll feel like I'm abandoning the story. Leaving it stranded."

"You're not going to do your writing, or yourself, any good if you continue this routine. I don't want to see you slide backward."

"I felt good when I was here, you say, just a few days ago. I was ready for changes for the good," Randy scowled. "What went wrong?"

"Maybe I shouldn't have revealed what I knew about Shawn. Possibly it was a burden rather than a blessing."

Doc could see by Randy's countenance that he was trying to straighten things out in his mind.

"I'd suggest a day off tomorrow. Hike, visit around. Maybe that will help clear the mist. Then proceed. Take some time to come up with a list of your desires. For heaven sakes, get out of that cabin every day."

"I know I want to complete the manuscript. Once I go home . . . I'm not coming back. I need my wife and family. They are number one on my list, they are my life and my future."

"Let's step back to plan number one. Walk and breathe in the spring mountain air. Your story will resurface."

The click of the door closing had Doc on the phone. Jill sounded frightened when she heard his voice.

"Not to worry, but Randy needs your presence. He needs you. . . . Hello?"

"The line isn't dead, Doc. I just wish those words had come from him."

"I don't want him to know I made this call. Send him a casual note telling him that you are planning a short visit. No kids allowed this time."

When Randy received Jill's note he was elated. His writing slipped to the back of his thoughts. Jill had written that she would arrive around four o'clock, on May 10th. He purchased potatoes to bake on the grill and two steaks. He had ingredients for a salad, and that could be Jill's part of the preparation.

• • •

A few days earlier he had gotten a note from Ginger Beal saying that she'd like to see him at his earliest convenience. It was quite a distance, but the walk would do him good. Leaving at ten o'clock gave Randy plenty of time before Jill's arrival.

Mrs. Beal ushered him inside Shawn's former apartment. It appeared that everything remained in place, as if Shawn would return at the end of the day. Randy didn't like being in this place.

A small box rested in Ginger's hand. "Mr. Tabano, I thought maybe your girl would like to have the necklace, as a remembrance. There was a friendship developing between her and Shawn. I am deeply sorry that it was not able to blossom.

"The other day I came to retrieve the necklace. It was then that

I discovered the tiny edge of a piece of paper sticking up from underneath.

"Shawn requested that if anything happened to her I was to sell her horse equipment and any other worthwhile belongings. She asked that the money be used to give your children free access to the horses here at the stable. It was her legacy. I honor it with great pride. Trish and Danny are welcome here anytime.

"No way would she have planned such a happening as her fall, Mr. Tabano. Not for herself, not for the horse. Her love for the horses was so very strong. I know there have been a few rumors about what happened, but I truly believe it was an accident. Since she did not wear the necklace that day, and she had every day after receiving it, possibly there was some kind of a premonition."

Randy turned away from her, facing the little window that looked out upon the horses in the paddock below. His shoulders shook.

A rough old hand touched his arm. "We have lost a dear friend. Let's let it go at that." She slipped the box into his pocket and walked away.

● ● ●

Randy's walk home was slow and miserable, but when he spotted their car in the drive he picked up speed. As he neared the cabin Jill came to the doorway with a fire-and-brimstone look that lessened his anticipation for seeing her.

"Where were you?"

"You said you'd arrive about four."

"Oh well, I left early."

They stared at each other in complete confusion. This was a game they had never played before.

Randy had set the table with the dishes that matched up the best and candles. He felt totally deflated. He rotated the potatoes until they looked great and he cooked the steaks to perfection. Jill tossed the salad. Neither bothered to light the candles. He had forgotten to buy dressing for the salad. They choked down their food in silence. Why was this happening?

Randy wondered if he had been away too long. Had love disappeared entirely? Maybe that's what he deserved.

Not long after they retired he silently rose and moved downstairs to the sofa.

The aroma of brewing coffee woke him. He sat up startled. Jill was preparing breakfast. Her eyes were swollen from crying. He wanted to touch her, to hold her close, but he was afraid. He tried to speak but no words came. They avoided eye contact. Finally Jill said, "I'm going to drive into town to pick up some additional groceries."

Randy kept running his hands through his hair. He picked up the dishes and washed them, cleaning the spattered grease spots on the stove.

Jill drove away. Randy showered and sat on the deck like a wilted wildflower. They never argued. They always discussed things openly. This routine was not to his liking.

He headed for the woods. After an hour he sat on a stump, exhausted, body and soul. "God, I'm sorry, but I'm not getting a clue here. Help me, us, somebody. Please do something. We are, mad, angry, falling apart. Whatever I've done, I ask forgiveness. This one is out of my hands. They say if it's too much turn it over to you. Hey, it's yours. I'll do whatever you want me to. I love her. I want my wife back. I'm not sure I even know who this woman is. Please help."

From his spot Randy could see the cabin in the distance. No car. Maybe she wasn't coming back. He spoke her name out loud. He did not hear her voice. Why had he remained silent, last night, this morning?

He stood up and followed a deer trail farther into the woods.

CHAPTER 33

Squatters Corners
Saturday morning, May 11, 2013

Knowing that Jill had arrived for her visit made Doc uncomfortable. Should he have interfered? It brought to mind his own wife. Maybe because he only remembered the good parts, he could never recall a misunderstanding between them. There most likely had been. Even so, he'd not search for the memory. The love and happiness was all he wanted to remember.

Doc was startled out of his daydreams by someone pounding on his back door. When he opened it Jill walked past him and sat down in a kitchen chair. He closed the door and turned back into the room to take a good look at her. His main thought was, "Oh dear."

Her first words were blurted out. "Is Randy seeing someone up here?"

Doc slumped down in the chair across from her. "Heaven sakes girl, where did you pick up a notion like that?"

"We have said only a few words, and he's not bothered to put his arm around me. We don't even look at one another."

"In the first place, missus, twice you have used the term 'we.' So, it's not a one-way street. Also if you arrived in this fighting mood and looked this disarrayed, I'd hesitate to chase after you, too." He smiled.

This brought her up short. Doc might as well have slapped her in the face, she looked so stunned. Slouching in the seat, her color drained away. She did look like a wreck.

Doc looked straight into her eyes. "Now, you want to talk about this in a civil manner? No more accusations?"

Jill took a long breath and her shoulders sagged even further.

Doc asked, "Have you told Randy the news yet?"

Jill's head jerked up. She squinted her eyes. "How do you know all this stuff? I'm not showing yet. How did you . . . ?"

Doc leaned on the table with his elbows. "I'm a doctor remember. There are faint tell-tale signs."

"It happened in March. I never thought to bring anything to prevent it from happening. We needed each other so badly that awful time."

"So what's the big blow-up?"

"For one thing, I'll be thirty-seven."

"That's not a difficulty these days."

Then the story spilled out. Doc listened intently. Finally Jill stopped talking. Doc reached across to all corners of the table and made like a motion as if gathering debris. He formed the pretend pile. Then packed it together like a snowball.

"So, leaving out the trivia, what I have sitting across from me is a pregnant woman who dearly loves her man, and if I guess right, wants to move the rest of the family here to Squatters Corner."

Jill's thinking process was working its way through what had happened since she rushed through the door.

"You are a clever fellow." She took a deep breath. "I failed the good-wife test, didn't I?"

Doc reached across and brushed the hair from her eyes.

"No, but I bet there is a man pacing back and forth in a cabin wondering what happened to his beautiful and loving wife. You say you haven't mentioned the news. Did you discuss wanting this to be the family's permanent home?"

"No, I can't figure why he hasn't had the courage to bring it up."

Doc held up his index finger. "Don't blow that black cloud up again. You just punctured it." He sat a minute in deep thought. "You know what Randy told me the other day? How homesick he was. That the book was not important enough to have you two and the children apart from each other. How once he left he wasn't ever coming back. He was going home." Both Doc and Jill sat back on that one.

"Randy hasn't talked much about his story line. He seems muddled."

Jill said, "The working title is *A Mountain Village*. I think the problem is that this place and its people have moved him so, and he's approached it upside down. He's taking facts and trying to turn them into a fiction story and it isn't developing to his liking.

"He can't guide the characters, so they are stumbling into each other. I understand his desire and concept but I think he needs to place the village in another location, and make up his usual unique characters."

"Why don't you talk to him about that? It may help him move his thinking in a new direction."

"What you're saying is, I should go home. I'm sure I owe you a fee."

"True, but I can't come up with a figure. Besides, it sounds like you will be a patient on a regular basis, so we'll get it straightened out." Doc patted her on the cheek. "*Go.*"

CHAPTER 34

Squatters Corners
Saturday afternoon and evening, May 11, 2013

After Jill left, Doc's thoughts turned back to Carl Miller. Carl had returned to good health by the end of February. Once he rediscovered his occupation he had been hired for numerous construction jobs. People in the surrounding area had heard about the fine work Carl did. He had recently been employed by a family twenty-five miles away to build a major addition to their home. Carl took great pride in his work, and should have.

The pounding Doc was hearing was taking care of a long-awaited wish. He had wanted bookshelves built in his bedroom, and Carl said it was the least he could do.

Yes, both Doc and Babs had drawn a breath of alarm when Carl had mentioned that he and Manda should find their own place. Doc enjoyed having Carl moving about in his house. Babs and her family had totally enfolded Manda into their routine. When Babs was working Doc's granddaughter looked after the little girl. Oftentimes Carl sat at the supper table and spent the early evening with his daughter and the little family she had adopted. When and if they did move on it would be a difficult adjustment for all of them.

One night in April as Doc was watching the evening news, he felt Carl watching him. He encouraged him to speak up.

"A question, Doc."

"Shoot."

"My wife died well over two years ago. I loved her very much. Am I being a bad person by being attracted to another young woman? Am I being unfaithful to Manda's mother?"

"Not at all. You're young and healthy. I would consider that a normal desire. Is it someone I know?" Carl's face turned pink. There was no immediate reply.

Then he asked a question that seemed more important to him than the first. "I don't want it to be just because she is taking care of Manda. That is not a good thing to base a relationship on."

Doc tried to keep his smile under wraps, but his eyes danced with delight.

• • •

A few days after his talk with Carl, Doc had been walking past Krismuses when he ran into Billy's grandpa.

"Hey Doc, I know that you will have a free minute for the yarn I have to tell." The two headed to Doc's kitchen where Gramps told the story.

After a family supper he, Billy, and Manda had gone to watch TV. A few minutes later Billy had headed toward the kitchen to get a drink. After barely stepping through the doorway Billy darted back to the TV. "Manda! My mom is sitting on your dad's lap and they are kissing each other."

With that Gramps had bolted out of the chair. Under his breath he mumbled, "It's about time. . . . Hey kids, we'd better go out and do our evening chores." When ushering them through the kitchen Gramps noticed that Carl was still seated and Babs was picking up the dishes. Billy gave the two a curious look. Manda walked up, and placing her little hands on Carl's knees, she explained, "We have to do chores now."

After that Carl did not come by the house for two days. On the third day he phoned and asked to speak to Gramps.

"You'll never believe it, Doc. He asked if it would be okay with me if he escorted Babs to a movie." The two men slapped each other on the back. By gosh, things were looking up in Squatters Corner.

• • •

Doc suddenly remembered that this was the night of the school social. He and Carl walked over together. They would meet up with Billy, Manda, Babs, and Gramps. The workers had done a fine job enlarging the cafeteria, and with Carl's help they had made some other improvements.

Carl and Doc stood talking with friends, then Carl began to peer around the room with an uneasy look. "Where's Manda?"

Babs pointed to a little girl sitting in a corner. The child was the right size, but she was not the plain little one Carl was searching for. She looked like a princess. Her hair was curled and hung on the shoulders of a beautiful white lace dress. She wore white socks with lace trim and white patent-leather shoes. The precious face with dark eyebrows and lashes, the pug nose, and perfect little lips belonged to his little Manda. Carl was astounded and stared in disbelief.

Carl sat down in a nearby gray folding chair. He followed the crease in his pants down from below his knee toward his ankle and back, between his forefinger and thumb.

Babs moved next to him. "I hope it's okay."

"I just didn't realize how pretty she was. I neglected that part. Guess I figured if she was clean and fed, loved and cared for we'd make it." He reached for Babs's hand and held it to his cheek. Doc and Gramps turned away. It seemed like it should be a private moment.

At that minute Manda spotted her dad. She jumped up and ran toward him, totally forgetting the cake and ice cream on her lap. Everyone attending the affair reached toward her as if it would help catch the cake as it fell. "Papa! Papa!"

On both her and the floor there was chocolate in abundance. It was a well-distributed finger painting. Just as Manda reached Carl she stopped and looked down. "Uh oh, made a mess." Babs took Manda's hand. "Let's go see what we can fix. Then you can give your dad a hug."

Manda looked into Carl's eyes. "Fix first, then hug. Fixed up special for you." Her innocent grin would have sold for well over a million bucks.

No one would know for several weeks that later that that evening Carl had asked Babs to marry him.

CHAPTER 35

Squatters Corners
Late Saturday afternoon, May 11, 2013

Randy was sure Jill did not just stop at the grocery or she would be back. Not knowing her whereabouts, he headed for the woods again. Sometimes the trees seemed like a place of worship to him. Maybe if he walked, some of this strangeness would drain away.

Had he neglected the home front because it was simpler to be here where there were few responsibilities? What kind of a man was he? Had he lost his courage for the rigors of everyday existence?

Then his thoughts turned a bend in the road.

During his time at Squatters Corner he had regained his belief in himself. It was because of Jill, Doc, Roy, Merry, Shawn, and others. And he must not eliminate his most powerful friend of all. The one who resides among the clouds but walks silently on earth. Although invisible, God had provided the means of rehabilitation.

Randy had learned that sometimes a person must give himself a lay-down day for some quiet time so that God can do God's work. He realized he had been pushing himself through walls of stress and not allowing God to enter his world. A quiet place with an open gate was his invitation, even if it only existed in his mind.

With these thoughts resurfacing, Randy turned back toward the cabin. He was standing by the stream when Jill pulled up in the car. His reflection in the rippling water, although obscure, was not of a man lost, but of a man of courage, a man moving in the right direction.

Jill walked slowly into the stream. Randy hoped his eyes passed the message to her. He was calm at last. God would help them see this through.

Jill did not look dejected anymore. "Maybe your pleasure island has disappointed you. Four deaths of people you knew well, happening in such a short time, turned it into a place like any other."

Randy studied her as she knelt down and reached in to scoop some clear water and let it run through her fingers. Then she moved to a rock and sat down. With a steady tone she talked on. "Frank said he'd sell the cabin to us for a good price. We'd have to put on an addition and install communication of course. I have checked out the schools. I have a job at Harris's concocting desserts."

Randy began to look around. "Is Ali Baba hiding nearby? Did I say 'Open Sesame'? Is this a joke? I can't believe this."

The shared thoughts of moving their lives to this outpost felt like fulfillment.

Randy was ready to jump the creek when Jill threw in the clincher. "Besides I think it would be nice to bring up our third offspring in Squatters Corner."

Randy walked right into the water and to where Jill was sitting. He was halfway to his knees in early spring water from the mountains.

"Now who's joking?"

"No one."

Climbing out of the frigid water Randy reached for Jill's hand. Slowly he pulled her to her feet and kissed her tenderly on the lips. Simultaneously they murmured, "I love you."

As they walked toward the cabin, so Randy could change into dry clothes and warm his feet, Jill began to laugh.

"Now what?"

"I will tell this child that he will recognize his father by his squeaky shoes, because he doesn't know enough to stay out of the stream in the spring."

Randy swung Jill around and kissed her again, not as tenderly as before. The message it conveyed was glorious. It held the promise of the future.

About the Author

Most of Donna's novels are set in Michigan where she was born 80 years ago. "Stories happen," says Donna, "walking everyday in the neighborhood. The houses begin to speak and the stories grow street by street, house by house."

Donna's oldest son asked her to take him on a walk and point out the elements of one of her novels. He was delighted as street names became names of characters, and as his familiar surroundings were sprinkled with his mother's magic storytelling dust!

The author welcomes correspondence from her readers:
P. O. Box 8231 Holland, Michigan 49422
DonnaBocks@gmail.com

About the Illustrator

Tom Ball has always loved to draw. He studied art and architectural drawing throughout high school. To relieve the intensity of his chosen profession in law enforcement, he draws. When the family goes camping, he sketches, and his daughter does too.

Tom is a two-time Olympian, having served on security details at both the Atlanta and Salt Lake City Olympics. He is the husband of Colleen, father of Travis and Sarah, and proud walker of Aspen, an English Springer Spaniel.

Connect with Donna and Purchase Her Books

Become a Facebook fan of Donna's:
facebook.com/DonnaBocksAuthor

Tweet Donna:
https://twitter.com/donnabocks

Order Donna's 7 novels:
www.amazon.com
www.lulu.com/spotlight/donnabocks
Kindle - www.amazon.com
Nook - www.barnesandnoble.com/c/donna-bocks
www.donnabocks.wordpress.com